A FRESH START]

Slick Rock 11

Becca Van

MENAGE EVERLASTING

Siren Publishing, Inc.
www.SirenPublishing.com

A SIREN PUBLISHING BOOK
IMPRINT: Ménage Everlasting

A FRESH START FOR TORI
Copyright © 2014 by Becca Van

ISBN: 978-1-63258-006-1

First Printing: October 2014

Cover design by Les Byerley
All art and logo copyright © 2014 by Siren Publishing, Inc.

Printed in the U.S.A.

PUBLISHER
Siren Publishing, Inc.
www.SirenPublishing.com

DEDICATION

Dear Readers,

I would like to thank you all sincerely for your continued support and hope you all enjoy reading about Tori and her men in Slick Rock, as well as catching up with some of the other characters.

Sometimes it's really hard to take the step and plunge back into life after being hurt but life is full of risks and if we never took chances we may never know how much we could be missing out on.

Wishing you all health, love and happiness.

Becca xxoo.

A FRESH START FOR TORI

Slick Rock 11

BECCA VAN
Copyright © 2014

Chapter One

"How's Rachel doing?" Luther Katz asked Ty Osborn as he leaned on the bar. His brothers, Jeremiah and Bryant, were on either side of him sipping on beers and listening to the conversation.

"Not so good." Ty frowned. "She's suffering badly with morning sickness."

"I'm sure you and your brothers are taking good care of her," Bryant said.

"Yeah, but the worst part is, other than making sure she eats when she can and that she stays hydrated, we can't do much else."

"I'll bet that's not true," Jeremiah piped up. "From what I saw the other night you guys make sure she rests when she's tired and won't let her lift a finger."

"She'd run herself ragged if we didn't watch her." Ty grinned. "She can be so damn feisty sometimes."

"Lucky bastard." Luther smiled.

"So what are your plans now that you've retired?" Ty asked.

"We're not sure yet. But we intend to settle in this town." Luther took a slug from his beer.

"You do?" Ty looked up from wiping the bar.

"Yep, we like the idea of sharing and when you e-mailed and told us about Rachel we talked about coming here after we got out of the Marines."

"You grew up on a ranch, didn't you?" Ty asked.

"That we did," Bryant replied.

"Have you thought about getting back to the land? There's always room for another cattle ranch," Ty said.

"We've thought about it, but we're not sure we could handle the slower pace," Jeremiah said.

"Why don't you see if you can hire onto one of the other ranches around here so you can decide?" Ty suggested.

Luther perked up at that suggestion and looked at his brothers. They both glanced at him and gave him a nod. "Can you introduce us to someone?"

"Sure." Ty nodded then scanned the patrons of the Slick Rock Hotel from behind the bar.

He nodded toward three big men at a table on the far side of the room and the two women with them. "That's Tom and Billy Eagle and Sheriff Luke Sun-Walker from the Double E Ranch. Tom and Billy own and run the ranch and Luke helps out on his days off from being Sheriff, as well as their wife, Felicity. Flick, as her men call her, is one of the best cowhands around, or she was until she got pregnant."

Luther eyed the black-haired beauty but then his eyes slid to the woman with long brown hair and his breath caught in his throat. He could only see her profile but from what he could see she was absolutely breathtaking. His cock twitched in his pants and he pushed off the bar and stood up straight. He'd never reacted that way to a woman before and he hoped like hell he wasn't looking at the other men's wife.

"Which one is Felicity?" Luther asked and heard the huskiness in his own voice. He just hoped Ty hadn't heard it, especially if he was ogling a woman that was off-limits.

"Flick has the black hair," Ty answered.

Luther glanced at his brothers and saw that they were looking as entranced as he was at the stunning brown-haired woman. Maybe working on the Double E Ranch looked better and better. He wanted to get to know the brown-haired beauty and hopefully go on a date with her, but first things first.

* * * *

Tori Springer had been in Slick Rock, Colorado, for a week and loved the small rural town so much she didn't want to leave. She was currently staying in the guest room on the Double E Ranch, visiting her good friend Felicity.

She hadn't seen Felicity in what felt like forever and after losing her job decided it was a prime opportunity to catch up with her friend. When she'd first heard that Felicity was in a ménage relationship with three men, Tori had been shocked, but the more Felicity told her over the phone the more envious she became. She would love to have one or more men showering her in love and affection. She'd watched the way Tom and Billy Eagle and Luke Sun-Walker interacted with Felicity, and often had to look away because of the love they shared. She wasn't really jealous of her friend, just…a little envious.

The two guys she'd gone out with had turned out to be jerks and she'd begun to think that all men were the same, selfish and egotistical. But not Felicity's men. She'd also seen other ménage trios and quartets interacting when she'd been out and about with Flick, as Felicity was affectionately called by her men, and wondered if there was something in the water or if the men of this town had just been brought up to protect, cherish, and take care of their women.

And the way those three big masculine men helped look after their two-year-old toddler, Carly Rose, was precious. Those men treated their daughter like a princess and she had her daddies wrapped around her little finger.

Tonight she, Flick, and Flick's husbands were going out for dinner to the local hotel and little Carly was being looked after by a sitter. Even though Tori was looking forward to a night out she was also a little nervous. There seemed to be more men than women in this town and they were all so big, muscular, and handsome. And although she loved looking at eye candy as much as the next woman, she didn't want to get involved with another man. Not that anyone had asked her. She wasn't full of herself, but she'd been told time and again that she was passably pretty. But she was done with men. She'd only broken up with her last boyfriend a month ago, and although she'd figured out she hadn't been in love with him, her pride had taken a battering. The asshole had been two-timing her and she'd found out through a mutual acquaintance. After kicking Rick to the curbside she'd vowed to steer clear of the opposite sex.

She glanced out the side window as Tom drove them all toward Slick Rock and took in the beautiful countryside. After living in a bigger town the appeal of the small country town was getting to her more and more. She'd even gone for a horse ride the other day, and even though she was a novice she loved it so much she wanted to learn to ride properly. She'd grown up with Felicity on the outskirts of Nampa, Idaho, and they hadn't been the best of buddies back then, but they had kept in touch. Felicity's grandma hadn't let her have people over to their ranch, and poor Flick never got to go anywhere other than school and home. She'd felt sympathetic toward her due to her harsh upbringing, but Felicity didn't need her sympathy anymore. Her friend was happy, content, and in love. She sighed at the thought of having a man of her own but then remembered her resolution to steer clear of anything with a penis, at least of the human variety.

Tori looked up when Tom slowed the truck and then parked in the parking lot outside the hotel. The place looked almost brand new or like it had recently been refurbished. She hoped they had a jukebox or a band playing later. Tori loved to dance and hadn't been out in such a long time. She'd spent most of her time working and hardly had a social life. Not that she went out a lot, but it was good to let her hair down now and then, and at the moment she had a hankering to let off some steam.

She had so many decisions to make and no clue in which direction she was going to take. Although she was pretty sure that she was in Slick Rock to stay. Lucky for her she didn't have many material things and when she'd ended the lease on her apartment in Nampa she'd sold what little furniture she'd had to the next tenant. Then she'd packed her small SUV with a few boxes and a couple of suitcases and headed here. Now she needed a place of her own and a job. She'd been a travel consultant before she'd been released due to the GFC. People weren't spending their money on things such as holidays or any other luxuries because of the economic downturn, but concentrated on surviving until the economy picked up again. Things were starting to turn around now, but it had been too little too late for her to keep her job.

She'd liked seeing how excited some people got as she helped them plan out their itinerary for their vacations. She loved seeing people happy, period. She got a kick out of seeing others joyful and that made her feel good inside.

Tori had thought of starting her own travel agency but didn't have the capital to do that. She doubted that this small town had a travel agent and hadn't thought to ask Felicity but planned to before the night was over. If there was an agent here maybe she could put in her resume and work there, but she wasn't holding her breath. Other than that she wasn't qualified for anything else, besides waitressing and working in a bar. She'd done that while she'd been going through college, much to her mother and stepfather's horror, and figured she wouldn't have any trouble doing it again. It would be like riding a bike. Once a girl learned she never forgot.

Tori smiled at Billy as he held the door open for her and then clasped her hand and helped her from the truck. That was another thing that astounded her. All the men of Slick Rock seemed to have nice manners and were courteous almost to a fault. Even the ranch hands on the Double E Ranch were chivalrous and that surprised her. Sure, she'd heard a few of them cussing but if any of the hands saw her they apologized immediately. None of the men in Nampa had given a shit about who was around when they let loose with swear words, not even children. And to her that was bad. It was okay to curse, but Tori didn't think it was right to blaspheme in front of the elderly or kids. Sometimes she thought she'd been brought up in the wrong era. She would have loved to have been around when the Wild West was alive and, well, where men were men and women were…women.

That didn't mean she didn't think that women weren't as capable as men, but respect from the opposite sex seemed to be more prevalent back then. Now no one seemed to give a damn about anyone else. Men and women included. Everyone was out for him or herself and didn't care who they hurt or trod on to get where they were going.

Tori felt more relaxed in the town of Slick Rock than she'd ever been, because she wasn't scared about being mugged or attacked in broad daylight. She had a feeling the men of this town would step right in if a woman was in danger, and that made her feel safe.

"Tori, are you coming?" Flick asked.

She gave Felicity a sheepish smile and followed her friend and her men inside. Billy walked behind her and again she had that sense of security. She really loved this town, or at least what she'd seen so far, and the people were so friendly. She hadn't encountered any of that in Nampa.

Billy helped to seat her across from Flick and then he took the seat to her left. Felicity was on her right and Tom and Luke were on Felicity's right.

"What would you like to drink, Tori?" Luke asked as he stood up again.

"White wine please."

Luke nodded, took the others' drink orders, and headed toward the bar with a smile. Just after he came back and handed the drinks out the waitress came over with the menus and handed them out. After glancing at the list, Tori decided on a chicken salad. The men talked about the ranch and Tori listened avidly. She loved seeing cowboys working with the animals. She loved watching them riding, roping and branding, because again it made her think of the Wild West.

After they'd finished their meal, Tori glanced around the large room. She saw the other ménage couples, but when she caught a few unaccompanied men looking at her she glanced away quickly.

"Who's that talking to Tyson at the bar?" Felicity asked her men, and Tori turned her head to look.

Her breath caught when she saw three very big, strong men leaning on the bar talking to the owner, Tyson.

"They must be their friends from the Marines," Luke said. "Damon told me they were coming to town and were going to check out the place. He thinks they want to settle in the country now that they've retired from service."

Tori couldn't help but look them up and down. She could see their faces in the mirror behind the bar and from what she could see they were all Adonises. Two of them had dark brown hair and the other had light brown hair. They looked to be tall even though they were slouching against the bar. When she saw the man near the end of the bar start to turn around she whipped her head back around and looked down at her nearly empty plate. For some reason she felt like he was looking at her. A shiver wracked the length of her spine and goose bumps broke out over her skin. The fact that she was reacting to a stranger, a man she'd never met before, worried her, because she'd never reacted this way to any man before, not even either of her exes.

Heat suffused her cheeks and even though she had the urge to turn around to see if he was looking at her, she fought it. There was no way she was going to meet the guy's gaze if he was looking this way and end up giving him the wrong impression. She'd learned from past experience that just meeting a guy's eyes could be misconstrued as a come-on, and that was the last thing she wanted. Tori was glad that Flick was talking to her men and didn't seem to be taking any notice of her. If her friend had picked up on her attraction she may well have tried to set her up. Felicity had already tried her hand in matchmaking with some of their ranch hands and it was embarrassing to have to say she wasn't interested. She hated the thought of hurting anyone, but it was better to take a stand so that problems couldn't arise in the future. Although she didn't think that the men had really been hurt when she'd refused their offers of dinner. How could they when they didn't even know her?

No, it was best to steer clear of any entanglements with men until she knew her own mind and had control of her life once more. How could she offer anyone anything when she didn't even have a job? Which reminded her...

"Is there a travel agent office in Slick Rock?" Tori asked.

"No," Luke replied. "Why? Are you thinking of opening up one of your own?"

"I've thought about it." She sighed. "But it's just not possible."

"Why not?" Tom asked.

"Because I don't have any money and now I don't have a job either." *Damn!* She hadn't meant to say that. She hadn't told Flick that she was unemployed and now she and her men knew. She hoped they didn't think she was here to freeload off of them.

"Tori, why didn't you tell me you'd lost your job?" Felicity reached out and patted the hand she had resting on the table.

"Because I won't be unemployed for long. I have every intention of getting another one."

"You could always go to the bank and get a loan. I'm sure you wouldn't have any trouble if you had a business plan," Billy said.

"Not in this economic downturn. Banks want to know that you have at least some money behind you as a deposit. I don't have anything."

"You won't know unless you ask," Tom said. "The economy is starting to pick up again. The banks may have loosened their rules a bit."

"You should go see a loan officer, Tori. You won't know for sure whether you can get a loan unless you ask." Felicity took a sip of her drink and then she was looking behind Tori.

Frissons of awareness raced up and down her spine and across her skin. Someone was behind her. Was it one of the three men she'd seen leaning against the bar? Maybe it was all three of them. *Please, don't let it be them. I'm not ready to get close to them or face them. I don't want them seeing how attracted to them I am. I'm not ready to deal with one man, let alone three.* Tori didn't want to look around and see who was behind her because she already had a pretty good idea who it was and didn't want to make a fool of herself, and end up drooling.

"Hey Ty." Luke smiled.

"Hi, this is Luther, Jeremiah, and Bryant Katz."

Tom, Billy, and Luke rose from their seats and shook hands with all the men. Tori kept her eyes on her half-empty glass of wine and hoped that none of them talked to her and that they wouldn't end up sitting at their table. She didn't know if she could keep her attraction to them from showing if they ended up any closer to her. She could still see their handsome faces in her mind's eye. And that wasn't all she could see. She'd seen the way the sleeves of their T-shirts stretched around their bulging biceps and how the denim jeans they wore cupped their delectable asses. Her heart rate and respiration escalated, the palm of her hands dampened with nervous excitement, and her girly bits stood up to take notice.

Shit, Tori, get a hold of yourself.

"Luther and his brothers are interested in starting up their own cattle ranch," Tyson said.

Tori had met Ty earlier when he'd come over to say hi to them so she didn't have to look to know who was speaking.

"Do you mind if we sit down and talk with you for a bit?"

Tori shuddered as the deep, gravelly, masculine cadence washed over her and more goose bumps formed on her skin. She hadn't realized that anyone was watching her until Felicity leaned over and whispered to her.

"Are you cold, Tori? Do you want to borrow my cardigan?"

"I'm fine." Tori mentally cursed the little tremor in her voice and hoped that no one had heard it. Felicity was looking at her intently and then a small smile graced her lips. She wondered what that was about but didn't dare ask. She only hoped that it wasn't because her friend had figured out about her attraction. The last thing she needed was Flick trying to match-make again.

"Grab some chairs and take a seat." Tom waved his hand to emphasize his statement.

"Come sit with me so there'll be more room, baby," Billy said right before he scooted his chair back, wrapped an arm around Flick's waist, and hauled her onto his lap.

Tori wanted to scoot across to Felicity's seat so she wouldn't end up hemmed in by two of the three men and was about to do just that, but then it was too late. One of the men was already sitting in the vacated chair. Tom and Luke moved their chairs and then another one was placed on her left side.

And then the introductions began. As much as she didn't want to look at the men she didn't want to be impolite, and when she met the gaze of the man on her right she sucked in a deep breath.

He was so damn fine with his dark brown hair, dark green eyes, and ruggedly handsome, chiseled features. Luther was the epitome of tall, dark, and good-looking.

"Pleased to meet you, Tori," Luther said.

Tori looked down at the hand he held out to her and she found herself reaching for it. When their hands connected and their skin slid together it was all she could do to stop the moan building up in her chest from escaping. She clenched her jaw and bit her tongue hard enough that she tasted blood, but she was able to stop from making any noise. When she finally found her voice, she was pleased that it didn't come out sounding like a squeak or breathy. "Hi."

She turned her head to the left and met blue-green eyes and took Jeremiah's hand when he offered it. He was so similar to Luther, yet his jaw was a little squarer and he had dark stubble along his jawline.

"Hey, Tori." Jeremiah's voice was deeper than Luther's but a lot smoother, and the touch of his hand sent heat traveling into her veins, too.

"Pleased to meet you," she managed to murmur.

Bryant leaned around Jeremiah and she looked into his blue eyes as he offered his hand. When more heat assailed her she was scared that her voice would tremble and so only nodded when he said 'hi' to her.

She was surrounded by three very big, brawny men and her body betrayed her by lighting up like the Fourth of July. They were older than her and looked confidant and more sophisticated and Tori just hoped she didn't do anything to make a fool of herself by showing her attraction. Not that she had any intentions of doing something about it, but it would be embarrassing if they knew she found them desirable and they didn't even find her attractive. But that was beside the point. She'd vowed to keep away from men and she was determined to keep her promise to herself. At least she hoped so.

She was glad when the men started talking about ranching and hoped that would keep any attention away from her. She thought about what Flick and her men had said about going to the bank and asking about a loan. The more she thought about it the more merit it had.

When she looked up she met Luther's green-eyed gaze and quickly looked away, but her eyes collided with blue-green eyes and she lowered her head until she was staring at the table top.

Tori felt their eyes on her even though she was no longer looking at them, and it wasn't just the two men sitting either side of her. Bryant was looking at her too. She began to fidget in her seat and when she realized she was panting slightly she knew she had to do something.

She shoved her chair back and muttered, "Excuse me," and hurried away toward the ladies' room, and was pleased to find it empty. She leaned on the counter and took deep breaths as she stared at herself in the mirror. Her cheeks were flushed, there was a definite sparkle in her eyes, and she could see her nipples pushing against her shirt.

"What the hell, Tori? Get control of yourself, girl." She turned the faucets on and ran cool water over her wrists, but it didn't seem to help to lower the heat running through her veins. "What makes them so special? You've seen handsome men before."

Yeah, but not as sexy, muscular, handsome, or sophisticated as those three men.

She turned off the tap and then reached for some paper towel and dried her hands and wrists. Just as she turned to walk toward the door it burst open.

"Are you all right, Tori?" Flick asked.

"I'm fine."

"You look a little flushed. Are you coming down with something?"

Yeah, you could say that. I would call it a case of plain old lust.

"No, I just felt a bit hemmed in." She wanted to slap her hand over her mouth when she said that, especially when a speculative look came into Felicity's eyes.

"They are something, aren't they?" Flick asked.

"Who?" Tori hoped that Felicity wouldn't see through her.

"The Katz brothers." Felicity tilted her head and then smiled. "You don't fool me, you know. I see that look on my face nearly every morning. You're attracted to them."

"No I'm not," Tori said a little too quickly and emphatically, and Felicity's grin got bigger.

"If you say so." Flick hooked her arm into hers and led her back toward the door. She paused with her hand on the handle and looked at her. "Have you finished hiding out?"

"Bitch," Tori muttered and Felicity burst out laughing.

"They like you, too."

"They do not!"

"Ah, yeah, they do. Maybe you could go out with them."

"Look, I don't want to get involved with anyone. Not for a long time. I've had it with men and want to concentrate on getting a job and a place to live."

"You can stay with us as long as you like, Tori. There's no need to have your own place."

"I appreciate what you're trying to do and thank you for it, but there is every need. I hate interrupting you and your husbands' lives. The sooner I get a job and my own place the better."

Felicity yanked open the door and they headed back to the table. Tori was glad she'd let the subject of the Katz brothers and her plans drop.

All the men stood up when they came back and didn't sit down until she and Flick were once more seated. She liked that the men all had such good manners. It made her feel special, which she knew was totally ridiculous, because as far as she was concerned she was no different than any other woman.

"What do you do Tori?" Luther had leaned down close to her ear so she could hear him over the music and chatter of the other people. Her pussy pulsed, leaking cream onto her panties, when his breath caressed her sensitive flesh.

"I'm currently out of work and looking for a job."

"What did you do?" Jeremiah asked from her other side, and when she turned her head he was so close that her lips bumped against his chin.

Damn. That small brush of her mouth made her lips tingle and she looked at his mouth, wondering if he would taste as good as he looked. When she realized what she was doing she turned back to the front, picked up her wineglass, and drained it before finally answering him. "I was a travel agent."

Bryant leaned forward and it was only then that Tori realized he'd been listening to the conversation. "Did you get to travel anywhere?"

She met his gaze for a heartbeat and looked away again. "No. I'd only been working for the firm for a year and was told I would have to prove myself before I got to do any travelling."

"Did you like it?" Luther asked.

"It had its ups and downs like any other job, I guess."

"What do you mean?" Jeremiah asked.

"Some of the people I dealt with were rude or treated me like I was a second-class citizen."

"Who would do that?" Bryant propped his elbow on the table as he turned toward her and rested his head in his hand. He looked kind of angry on her behalf, but those thoughts drifted from her mind as she gazed at him again.

He was so damn hot just like his brothers and she was having trouble keeping her eyes off all three of them. They were older than her and she felt way out of her league talking with superior, confident men. And the more they asked questions the more tense she became.

"Well-off people mostly. There were a couple of well-to-do families in our town"—*including my own stepfather and cold-hearted bitch of a mother*—"and whenever they came in they always seemed to look at me down their noses. It pissed me off, but there was nothing I could do about it, especially if I wanted to earn a commission. But there were some really nice people too and they made up for the snobby ones."

"You sound like you didn't really enjoy your job too much, Tori," Luther said. "Have you thought of doing something else?"

Tori frowned. As a little girl she had always dreamed of traveling, and as she grew up she'd thought the best way to achieve that goal was get into the travel agent business. But now, looking back over the year she had worked for the agency, she realized she hadn't really enjoyed her job. Had she made a mistake taking courses at college in business and tourism? Should she have chosen something else? But what made her a little trepidatious was the fact that Luther had picked up on her emotions, when he didn't really know her.

How the hell did he do that?

All of a sudden she had an epiphany. It wasn't the travel that had enticed her to do that course and take that job. Tori had never been accepted for who she was and she realized that she had been looking for a place to belong. Somewhere she would fit in, where she wasn't perceived as an anomaly.

She pushed those disconcerting thoughts aside came back to the subject. She'd always wanted to own her own business and had been working toward getting the experience she needed to achieve what she wanted out of life, but now it seemed it was time to rethink her career choice.

"I don't know," she finally answered Luther.

"How old are you, honey?" Jeremiah asked.

"Twenty-four." Tori scowled at him and then reciprocated in kind. "How old are you?"

Jeremiah's lips tilted at the corners and then he laughed. The smile made him even more handsome, and the sound of his deep laughter shot straight to her clit and pussy.

Shit! I am in so much trouble.

"I'm thirty-four." Jeremiah chuckled again.

Luther tapped her on the shoulder to get her attention and she gulped when she saw the humor in his eyes. "I'm thirty-five, just in case you're wondering."

"And I'm thirty-two," Bryant said and stared at her intently.

She looked at Jeremiah when he started talking again and hoped her face wasn't as red as it felt.

"You're young enough to do anything you want to do." Jeremiah took a swig from his beer. "Maybe coming to Slick Rock was meant to be."

When she realized she was gawking at the way his throat muscles and Adam's apple moved as he took another drink and swallowed, she quickly looked away again. Had she been reading too much into the look he gave her? Was that heat and appreciation she'd seen in his eyes as he perused her body over?

No, Tori, don't even go there, girl. There is no way those three hunky, sexy men see you in anyway other than Felicity's friend.

At least I hope that's the case.

Chapter Two

Jeremiah's cock was as hard as a rock. From the moment he'd seen Tori from across the room he'd been drawn to her just as his brothers had. But when he'd sat down next to her and smelled the light strawberry scent on her warm skin he'd had a boner. When he'd seen her from over near the bar he'd thought she'd been pretty, but now that he was seeing her up close he realized that had been a gross understatement.

Tori was gorgeous with her long brown hair, aquamarine-colored eyes, and slim yet curvaceous body. When he'd first sat down and seen her beautiful face he'd been worried she was too young for him and his brothers. Even though they were older than her it wasn't an insurmountable gap.

Thank you, God.

Eleven, ten, and eight years weren't too much of a difference. *Please, don't let it be too much of a gap for her.* She was over twenty-one, fully grown, and hopefully as attracted to them as they were to her. Tori was old enough to make her own decisions, and he just hoped that she wouldn't be averse to having three older men courting her.

She'd been gazing down at the table since he'd spoken last and had a frown on her face as if she was thinking. He wondered if she was pondering over what he'd said about what she was going to do, or if she was pissed at him for saying she was young. Women were funny creatures at times and didn't like to be told they were too young or too old. Some women hated being told what to do at all. He speculated if she was one of them.

Finally she lifted her head and went to take a sip from her empty wineglass but put it down again when she saw that it was already gone. Jeremiah had snagged her glass and risen to his feet before she could blink. "What are you drinking, beautiful?"

He had to hold in a smile when she gaped at him and then quickly shut her mouth again. Her lips pulled in tight and she frowned as if he had insulted her, but then her face lost all expression.

"White wine please."

As he stood waiting to be served, he watched Tori and then cursed under his breath when he saw Bryant move across into the chair he'd been sitting in. Not that he really blamed his younger brother for wanting to be close to a gorgeous woman, but he'd been hoping to talk with Tori more. Then he thought that maybe it wasn't such a bad idea that Bryant was sitting next to her. He was more lighthearted and the jokester of the three of them. If anyone could get Tori to loosen up, Bryant could. The more questions he and Luther had asked the more tense Tori seemed to get.

He didn't like it that she was uncomfortable around them. Maybe it was because she was new to town, too.

"What'll you have, Jer?" Ty asked and Jeremiah gave the order. Minutes later he had paid Tyson and was making his way back to the table with a full tray in his hands. After passing out the drinks he sat in Bryant's chair.

"Okay." Tom leaned back in his chair and grabbed Felicity's hand in his. "When do you three want to start working on the ranch?"

Jeremiah looked to Luther, then Bryant, and back to Luther again before nodding at his older brother.

"How about tomorrow?" Luther asked.

"Sounds good to me."

"Where are you guys staying?" Felicity asked.

"In the motel down the street," Jeremiah answered.

"We have two lots of bunkhouses. One of them isn't being used."
Felicity looked at Tom and then Billy before resting her gaze on Luke
and then looked at Tom again.

Tom lifted up Felicity's hand and kissed the back of it before
giving her a nod and a grin.

"That settles it." Felicity smiled. "You'll stay in the vacant
bunkhouse."

"Thank you, ma'am. We appreciate that," Luther said and nodded
his head.

Jeremiah mentally rubbed his hands together. Now he and his
brothers would be close to Tori all the time. Hopefully they could get
her to go out on a date with them and they could court her from then on.

He hated that Tori had had to deal with people who looked at her as
a second-class citizen. He' seen the anger and pain in her eyes when
she talked about them. He had a feeling there was more to that story
than she let on and wanted to delve deeper into her psyche but he didn't
think she'd appreciate him asking too many questions. She seemed to
be really uptight right now and didn't want her feeling anymore
uncomfortable than she already was. Hopefully as they got to know her
and she them, she would relax and open up with them more.

* * * *

Bryant glanced up from the calf he was branding when he caught
movement out of the corner of his eye. He and his brothers had been
working on the Double Eagle Ranch for two weeks now and they all
knew that this was what they wanted to do with their lives.

He watched the sway of Tori's hips as she walked away from the
house toward the gazebo and hoped that he would get to talk with her
more tonight. Ever since they had been on the ranch she had tried to
avoid them, and he wondered if they intimidated her. He and his
brothers were at least a foot taller than her and a lot of women seemed

wary of their size. It seemed that Tori wasn't the exception in that respect.

She had become more closed off since they had been staying in the bunkhouse, and even though he and his brothers tried to get her to talk with them she only ever answered with one-word answers.

Last night after dinner with everyone, he'd gone out onto the verandah to relax. Tori had been sitting on one of the chairs and staring off into space. Bryant had leaned back against the railing and surreptitiously watched her. He saw her glance toward him and then she had shivered and he wondered if she felt the attraction too. When he'd started asking her questions her whole body had tensed up.

"How are you, Tori?"

"Good."

"Have you decided what you're going to do?"

"No."

"Do you like living in Slick Rock?"

"Yes."

Bryant sighed with frustration as he looked her body over and when his eyes alighted on her face again, he watched her cheeks turn pink. *Is she looking at me from under those lowered eyelashes?* When her lashes fluttered and her face turned a darker shade of pink, he knew she was. That was when he knew she felt the attraction, too. But how were he and his brothers supposed to court her when she wouldn't even talk to them?

Trying to get her to talk was like pulling teeth. He'd been about to ask her if she was going to live in Slick Rock permanently but she had risen to her feet, glanced at him before looking away quickly, and after saying "Good-night" had scurried inside.

He was becoming more and more exasperated, and he got to thinking that just maybe she had been hurt by a man before. If that was the case and she didn't give them the time of day then he couldn't see how they could form a relationship with her.

Each weekday for the past two weeks he'd seen her driving out, and he wondered if she was looking for a job or maybe a place to live. He didn't want her leaving the ranch because then he and his brothers wouldn't be able to see her every day. Meal times were the only times they got to be near her, and he'd miss that if she left. Bryant relished each and every second he spent in her presence. He and his brothers took turns sitting next to her, on either side of her. Whenever they could, they brushed up against her as they passed over the platters of food. When he handed over the bowl of mashed potatoes last night their fingers had brushed and she practically snatched the bowl out of his hand. He'd looked at her with a frown but she was determined not to meet his eyes, but then he'd noticed the goose bumps on her arm and her nipples had been standing to attention.

What worried him and his older brothers was the way she seemed to clam up whenever they were around. He'd heard her talking to Felicity and her men without any hesitation and even a couple of the ranch hands. That pissed him off big time.

Bryant knew he was being an ass to think that way but he was concerned that one or more of the ranch hands would woo her before he and his brothers could. She was aware of them in every way but seemed hell-bent on ignoring them.

"Bryant, get you mind back on the job," Luther snapped at him.

He wasn't the only one frustrated with Tori. She seemed to go out of her way to thwart every minute they spent with her and although he wanted to chase after her and throw her over his shoulder and carry her away so he could kiss her senseless, he wouldn't. If she'd been hurt before the last thing he wanted to do was scare her off even more.

Bryant branded the calf. Luther let it go and he watched as it scrambled to its feet and went running to the other side of the corral. He loved the physical work and how his body felt tired after a hard day, but the best thing was that he could let his guard down. He'd only spent seven years in the Marines, not as long as his older brothers, but it was a relief knowing he didn't have to sleep with one eye open anymore, or that he couldn't be called away to some hell hole on the other side of the world to fight in a war that seemed to be never ending.

He and his brothers had seen some bad things while serving their country, and they all suffered from nightmares. Bryant was glad that they weren't sleeping in the main house where they could disturb the others if they woke up yelling. Sometimes he wondered if it was a good idea to settle down with a woman when they were all still dealing with shit, but he was sick and tired of being alone. The thought of going out and hooking up with a woman for a quick lay left him cold.

Bryant wanted what Tom, Billy, Luke, and Felicity had, and he wasn't about to indulge in meaningless sex just for the sake of getting his rocks off. Besides, there was only one woman he wanted, and he wasn't giving up until he could find out if they were all compatible in every way. Tori Springer was the woman he wanted, and he wasn't about to settle for anyone else.

* * * *

Tori glanced toward the corral and nearly moaned when she saw Luther, Jeremiah, and Bryant branding the cattle. She loved watching the way their muscles rippled and bulged beneath their shirts as they worked. As she walked toward the gazebo her cell phone vibrated and she wondered who was texting or calling her. The only friend she had was Felicity and her mom and new stepfather were too wrapped up in each other to care about what she was doing. They'd virtually wiped their hands of her when she'd started working part-time in high school and then told them she was going to pay her own way through college. Frank had pitched a fit, ranting and raving at her that he was more than capable of paying for her tuition, but Tori didn't want to feel like she owed him anything. Frank was sly and she didn't like him at all. She had a feeling that he would hold the fact he'd paid for her schooling over her head and tell her she owed him. And she hadn't been wrong to think that way. Frank played mind games and was more than a little paranoid, but she could see through him and had realized from the time she'd turned fifteen that her stepfather was a greedy, selfish bastard and always had his eye on the main goal. Power, money, and himself. Although, he seemed to treat her mother with respect even if he didn't seem to be very loving toward her. But she could see that her mom was in love with the asshole.

Not that she begrudged her mom having a relationship. In fact she was glad her mother had found someone to love after her husband, Tori's father, had died in an accident so long ago. But what did hurt and made her angry was that her mom didn't seem to care about her anymore. She'd met Frank when Tori was only five years old, and from then on Tori felt like she'd been pushed aside.

Frank was a rich man, and even though he had paid for all her high school education, fed, and clothed her, he had hardly ever acknowledged that she was around unless it was for his own purposes. Her mom had become more distant with each passing year, and by the time Tori had finished high school she couldn't wait to get out of the cold mausoleum she had been living in.

She only vaguely remembered the small house she and her mom had lived in when she was little, but that house had been so full of love. Her mom had changed into an emotionless woman and Tori often wondered if it was Frank's doing or the fact that her mother thought she was now better than anyone else since she was married to a man that had a lot of money.

She glanced at the screen on her phone and sighed. It was her mother calling, and even though she loved her mom she didn't like her very much and didn't really want to talk to her. Her mother only ever contacted her now if she wanted something, not to see if she was okay. But she knew if she didn't and her mother had to leave a voice mail message, she would never hear the end of it, so she answered.

"Hi, Mom."

"Tori, I just thought I'd let you know that Frank and I are going on a worldwide trip. Frank's taking me to Europe and I don't know when we'll be back."

"That's nice," Tori said. "I hope you have a good time."

"I was hoping you'd given up the idea of staying with your little friend in the country and come back home. Frank would really like to have you taking care of the house."

The "house" was a fucking twenty-bedroom mansion that had a contingency of servants living in servant's quarters and there was no way in hell Tori was going to stay in that museum for any length of time.

"I can't, Mom. I'm happy where I am and I'm looking for a job."

"There is no need for you to work, Tori. You know Frank frowns at that sort of thing."

I don't give a shit what Frank thinks or wants.

"Please, Tori."

"No, Mom. I can't."

The silence on the other end of the line was almost deafening. Then she heard her mother's cold voice again.

"You disappoint me, Tori. I don't know why I bother with you. This was your last chance, young lady. You'll never be reasonable, will you? You're no longer my daughter."

A click sounded in Tori's ear and she sank down onto one of the seats in the gazebo. She didn't even realize that she was crying until a teardrop plopped onto her hand. She inhaled raggedly and wiped the moisture from her cheeks. She knew she shouldn't have answered the call. It was always the same. Her being a disappointment to her emotionless, stuck-up mother and snobby stepfather. She'd never felt like she really fit in with anyone and didn't see that changing anytime soon.

Felicity was her only friend, and as much as she loved staying with her on the ranch, she was cramping her and her husbands' life. She felt like a third wheel, but that was nothing new. Nothing had changed since she was five years old, so why would now be any different?

It was time to *do* instead of procrastinate. She would get a job while she tried to figure out what she wanted to do with her life and also find a place to live. That would be a start.

Tori wiped her cheeks and eyes again to make sure none of her tears showed and hurried back to the house. First she would search online for a job, and if that didn't work she would walk the length of Slick Rock handing out her resume. Surely she could find somewhere to work.

She walked into the kitchen and found Felicity making a cup of coffee. "Do you want a cup?"

"Yes please. Would it be okay if I used the computer in the office?"

"Sure. You don't have to ask, Tori." Felicity handed her a mug of coffee.

"Thanks." Tori hurried to the office, knocked on the door in case someone was in there, and entered when no one answered. Minutes later she was perusing job sites. There wasn't much to be found and she began to wonder if she'd made a mistake coming to Slick Rock. Maybe she should have moved to a larger town or city instead. She leaned back in the chair and sighed.

Felicity came into the study with Carly and sat down with the little girl on her lap. She was so precious with her black curly hair, sleep-flushed face, and soft skin. Tori felt a yearning so deep and profound to hold her own child it was painful.

"Did you find anything?" Felicity asked as she pointed at the computer monitor.

"No."

"Don't worry so much, Tori. Something will come up. Please promise me you won't leave here just because you feel you're infringing on our privacy, because that isn't the case at all. And don't you dare say you feel like a freeloader. God, you have been doing all the cleaning and most of the cooking."

"I like to help out. I can't just sit around and do nothing. I'm used to working and would get bored if I sat on my ass all day long."

"I appreciate everything you've been doing. This one keeps me on my toes and I am going to get more tired with another baby on the way."

"You're pregnant?"

Flick smiled and nodded.

"Oh my God. Congratulations." Tori leaned over and, being careful she didn't squish Carly, hugged Felicity. "I'm so happy for you all."

Tori moved back in her chair and when Carly put her arms out to her and demanded "up" she lifted her into her arms and cuddled the sweet-smelling toddler on her lap.

Felicity covered her mouth when she yawned. "God, I hate how tired I am through the first trimester. And I'm going to have to go shopping for more baby clothes and another car seat, and more maternity wear. The closest town for that stuff is in Gateway and that's nearly two hours away."

"That's quite a drive." Tori rubbed her cheek against the top of Carly's head and looked at Felicity when she yawned again. "Why don't you go and take a nap? I can take care of Carly. Can't I, precious?"

"Auntie Tori," Carly whispered and snuggled her face in between Tori's boobs.

"Are you sure?" Flick asked. "She's not quite awake yet, but when she gets going she doesn't stop."

"I know. I've taken care of her before."

"So you have." Felicity chuckled. "I guess once you're a mom you never stop worrying. Thank you. I will take you up on that. Come and wake me in an hour or if she gets to be too much."

"We'll be fine, won't we, precious?" Carly nodded her head, peeked up at her, and gave her a mischievous grin.

Felicity smiled again, got to her feet, and headed to her room for a nap.

"Do you want a drink, Carly?"

"Yes."

"Yes what?"

"Yes pwease."

"Good girl. Let's go then." Tori stood up and carried Carly into the kitchen. She got her a drink of water and gave her a banana when she said she was hungry. After checking to see if she had a nappy on or her big girl pants and made sure the little girl was dry, she took her to the toilet, and after washing their hands they went outside.

"Horsies, Auntie Tori." Carly looked up at her and clutched her hand tighter while pointing with her free hand to the corral.

"You like the horsies, don't you, Carly?"

"Yes. Want to ride."

"Not today, sweetheart. I can't ride very well and it would be too dangerous. Do you want me to push you on the swing?"

"Swing. Wee." Carly giggled and tugged her in the direction to the swing set at the opposite end of the house.

Tori breathed in the fresh spring air and realized it wouldn't be long before summer was upon them. It was heating up quickly and today was quite warm. She was glad she had stopped to put the little cowgirl hat on Carly's head to protect her from getting burnt. Just as they neared the swing Tori heard a rattle and without stopping to think she swept Carly up into her arms, held her against her chest, and froze. She was too scared to move her body but scanned the ground nearby and her eyes lit onto the snake curled up at the base of the swing set no more than two meters away.

"Auntie Tori…"

"We're going to play a game, Carly," Tori whispered but all the while kept her eyes on the snake. "We are going to see who can stay still and quiet the longest. If you win I will buy you an ice cream."

"I loved ice screen. I loved choc'late the bestest."

"You have to stay very still and quiet to be able to win the game and get your ice cream. Can you do that, precious?"

"Yes."

Carly wrapped her little arms around Tori's neck and hugged her tight, but she must have seen the snake when it rattled its tale.

"I don't like snakes, Auntie Tori. I want my daddies."

"I know, sweetie. I want your daddies too."

"Are you scareded, Auntie Tori?"

"No, just a little nervous."

"I scareded."

Don't worry, Carly Rose. I won't let that snake get you." Tori could feel Carly trembling and even though she wanted to move away, she was shaking too and didn't think her legs would hold her if she tried to step away. Plus, if she did move, the snake would probably strike and then she would be in a world of trouble.

Carly Rose shifted in her arms and then she screamed so loud she hurt Tori's ear. She couldn't work out what the little girl said until she screamed again.

"Daddies, get de snake." Carly Rose started wailing loudly and no matter what Tori said she couldn't calm the little girl down.

Tori heard footsteps pounding fast and hard as more than one man ran toward them and sighed with relief as she rubbed Carly's back.

"Cover your ears with your hands, Carly," Luther ordered, but the little girl was so intent on her crying she either didn't hear or didn't understand what he wanted her to do.

Tori gently pushed Carly's face against her chest and then used her hand to cover the ear not against her body.

"Don't move, sweetheart," Jeremiah ordered and then a loud gunshot sounded and Tori couldn't help but flinch.

She watched the snake fly apart and writhe on the ground in the throes of death, and even though she knew it was safe to move she couldn't seem to get her body to cooperate with her brain.

"Are you okay, sweetie?" Jeremiah came into view and Tori realized he was talking to her and not Carly like she first thought.

Tori nodded her head and gulped.

"Give Carly to me, darlin'." Bryant reached out and took Carly out of her arms and then Tori was being swept off her feet.

Tori squeaked and then looked up into Luther's green eyes.

"You're okay, Tori. You're safe now."

Tori nodded and rested her cheek against his shoulder. Her heart was still pounding in her chest, and being this close to him didn't help any to calm her down. She could smell the scent of his manly sweat and the woodsy cologne, body wash, or soap he'd used that morning, and no matter how hard she tried she couldn't stop herself from breathing him in again, and again, and again.

"What's going on?" Tom asked as he hurried over to Carly and took her from Bryant's arms.

"There was a rattler near the swing set. We had to shoot it. It looked like it was getting ready to strike."

"Shit."

Carly stopped crying and immediately copied her father.

"Carly Rose, you know you're not supposed to say bad words." Tom was looking at his daughter and even though he didn't smile, Tori could see the amusement in his eyes.

"Daddy said a bad word."

"Yes, I did. I'm a very naughty daddy and I won't be saying that again when little ears are around."

"Der was a big snake, Daddy. Auntie Tori pickeded me up so it wouldn't get me."

"Auntie Tori was very brave."

"We playeded a game, Daddy. She told if I winned I could get a choc'late ice screen."

"What was the game?"

"I had to be real quiet and stay stilled. I did didn't I, Auntie Tori."

"Yes you did, precious girl." Tori wasn't about to remind the little girl she'd screamed her head off. She was just glad that they were both safe and the snake was dead. "I'll have to go to the store so you can have your chocolate ice cream after you've eaten all your dinner like a good girl."

"Daddy, I want Mommy."

"Mommy will be down soon, Carly, but she's having a nap right now." Tom and Carly disappeared inside and it was only as their voices faded that Tori realized she was still in Luther's arms.

"I'm fine. You can put me down now." Tori looked up at Luther as he sat down on the porch steps and placed her in his lap. When she went to get off, he wrapped an arm around her waist and then nudged her chin up with a knuckle beneath her jaw.

"You scared the crap out of us, baby."

"How do you think I felt?" Tori looked to either side of her when Jeremiah and Bryant sat on the step on either side of her and Luther. She turned her head and dislodged the hold he had on her chin and tried to get up again. And again Luther stopped her.

"Why are you fighting this attraction, Tori?" Jeremiah asked.

She'd had enough of being restrained and shoved at the thick forearm across her stomach. "I don't know what you're talking about." Tori scrambled off Luther's lap and took a couple of steps away from the three Katz brothers, and then she turned to face them.

"You keep telling yourself that, darlin'." Bryant cocked an eyebrow up. "You may just start believing it if you tell yourself enough times."

The move was so sexy and masculine, her body started to respond. Her breasts swelled, her areolas ruched, and her nipples hardened. But what was worse was the way her pussy clenched and dripped cream onto her panties. She turned her back to them and tried to get her wayward arousal under control.

Tori walked away from them and didn't once look back. She heard them whispering behind her but didn't try to work out what they were saying. She wasn't interested in the least.

Maybe she would eventually believe it if she told herself often enough.

Tori rolled over in bed and tried to push the Katz brothers from her mind. Every time she closed her eyes they were all she could see and she was having trouble going to sleep. She blanked her mind and envisaged looking at a black screen, and sighed when she finally felt her muscles relaxing.

Tori moaned as Luther's tongue slid against hers. The mewl that escaped her mouth as another mouth latched onto one of her hard, aching nipples was muffled by Luther's kiss. Three pairs of hands swept and caressed over her naked body causing her to shiver and goose bumps to form on her skin.

She cried out when fingers caressed her wet pussy lips and then delved into her folds.

Luther broke the kiss and stared deeply into her eyes. "You like it when we kiss and touch you, don't you, Tori?"

"Yes," she moaned.

Bryant released one nipple before moving his head to the other and laving the tip with his tongue before drawing it into his mouth.

Jeremiah nudged her legs further apart and then began nibbling and licking his way up the inside of her thigh. The closer he got to her pussy the more her cream seeped out. The flames smoldering inside her began to flame hotter and brighter and no matter how hard she tried to calm her breathing, it didn't help. She was panting and shaking with need and the more they touched and kissed her the more she shook with desire. When Jeremiah licked his tongue up from her dripping pussy hole to her clit she was lost.

The more they touched her, the more she needed their hands on her and the hungrier she grew.

Tori arched her hips up pushing her cunt into Jeremiah's mouth and he chuckled against her pussy sending vibrations down deep inside.

Bryant lifted his mouth from her nipple, slanted it over her lips, and kissed her rapaciously, wildly, deeply.

Luther pinched and plucked at one nipple while taking the other one into his warm, wet mouth.

"You taste fucking delicious, honey. I could eat you out all day long," Jeremiah said just before lowering his head back to her pussy.

"Oh." Tori was overwhelmed with arousal and the sensations running through her body as they loved on her, but it still wasn't enough to appease the famishment traveling through her veins.

Jeremiah rimmed her weeping vagina with his finger and then he slowly pushed it up and inside of her as far as it would go. He pumped it in and out a few times before adding a second finger. With each press forward he increased the pace of his thrusting digits and the tension inside her built along with the pleasure beginning to consume her.

Bryant slowed the kiss and lifted his head at the same time Luther removed his mouth from her nipple.

"Turn her onto her side," Luther commanded, and between him and Bryant they rolled her over.

Jeremiah's mouth stayed latched onto her pussy but he removed his fingers from her cunt as he lifted one of her legs up high. He shifted on the bed and then his fingers were stroking in and out of her again.

Tori cried out when a cool lubed finger rubbed over her anus and she turned to look at Luther over her shoulder, but Bryant gently clasped her face in his hands and started kissing her again.

Bryant released her lips, lay down on the bed so that his body was sort of curving around the top of her head, and thrust his hips forward. Tori eyed the glistening drop of fluid in the slit of his hard cock and then she stuck her tongue out and licked it off.

"Yes, Tori. Suck my cock, darlin'."

Just as she took his cock into her mouth Luther breached her ass with his finger. She moaned and sucked harder on Bryant's cock.

"That is so fucking hot. You're so fucking sexy, baby," Luther rasped against her ear. "You like having my finger in your ass, Jeremiah's in your pretty little cunt, and my brother's cock in your mouth, don't you?"

"Hmm," Tori hummed.

Jeremiah began pumping his fingers in and out of her faster, harder and deeper as he licked and sucked on her clit. Luther added another finger to her ass counterthrusting to Jeremiah and she bobbed up and down over Bryant's cock.

The fire inside her was now burning out of control and her internal muscles began rippling as the tension inside grew and her pussy walls got closer and tighter.

Tingles raced through her veins and her whole body began to tremble. And then she was right on the cusp of something so exquisite it almost frightened her.

Tori screamed as the coil that had been winding tighter inside her snapped and sent her hurtling up into the clouds. Her muscles contracted around the fingers still pressing in and out of her ass and pussy. Her cunt clenched and let go, clamped down and released causing her whole body to quake and quiver.

Tori came awake with a gasp. He pussy was still emitting aftershocks and her panties felt sticky.

"Oh. My. God." Tori flung the covers aside and sat up on the side of her bed. She covered her hot face with her hands and moaned. "You are in so much trouble, girl. How the hell am I going to be able to look at them let alone be near them after fantasizing about them?"

She pushed to her feet and headed into the bathroom. "Damn it to hell."

Chapter Three

Another week had gone by and Luther was getting more frustrated as each day passed. Tori disappeared every day and the only time he or his brothers saw her was at night. He wanted to ask her where she'd been, who she'd been with, and what she was up to. But he didn't have the right. And that irked him more than anything.

He, Jeremiah, and Bryant had tried to get her to open up with them, but she remained closed up tighter than a chastity belt locked around the hips of a virgin. He'd tried talking to Tom, Billy, and Luke. They didn't know much and suggested they talk to Tori, but they hadn't had a chance to speak to her alone. They were all busy working the ranch, and Felicity had her hands full with her daughter, as well as dealing with another pregnancy.

He and his brothers wanted to be able to court Tori, but she was avoiding them and there was no way they would be talking to her when others were around. Luther couldn't wait for tomorrow. It was Saturday and hopefully Tori wouldn't be going anywhere. He was determined to get her alone, even if he had to hogtie her, sling her over his shoulder, and carry her off. But if he did that would she avoid them even more? Fuck, he was so messed up. The woman he and his brothers thought could be their one and only didn't want a bar of them and he had no idea why or what to do about it. But at least there was one certainty in their lives.

He and his brothers knew for sure that they wanted their own ranch. They planned on looking for a place to buy and then purchase some cattle. He wanted to have the best damn beef in the country, or at least as good as what they had here on the Double E Ranch, but instead of having grain-fed beef, Luther wanted his cattle to be raised on totally organic and pesticide-free feed. It would take a lot of hard work, but then everything worth doing was worth doing properly.

Maybe he and his brothers should plan a picnic or something and ask her out, but he wasn't sure she'd agree. He was so damn frustrated at the way she kept thwarting them.

She was a stubborn little thing. He knew that she knew they wanted to talk to her and be with her. Tori was a wonderful, capable, beautiful, sexy woman. She'd taken over most of the house chores from Felicity and, man, could she cook, but she always scurried away after a meal was finished. Even though he and his brothers had tried to collar her in the kitchen, the house was too busy to give them time to talk to her privately.

Two nights ago he'd walked into the kitchen as Tori was beginning to put the roast beef and vegetables onto serving plates. She'd been trying to reach a platter in one of the overhead cupboards and couldn't quite reach it. Luther had come up behind her and as he got the plate down he'd placed his hand on her hip. She'd frozen at his touch but he'd felt the shiver wrack her body and knew she was just as aware of him in a sexual way as he was of her. When she'd turned around her face had been totally devoid of expression. She'd met his eyes briefly before looking away again and muttered thanks as she'd put more distance between them.

"You're welcome, sexy."

She'd glared at him as if she was annoyed but her eyes had told a completely different story. There had been desire in them when she met his before glancing about the room but then she'd opened her mouth. "You're interrupting me. If you don't need anything why don't you go and wait in the dining room with the others?"

Although she'd posed it as a question it had come out as a demand.

Luther had moved in close until he could feel the heat from her body and smell her feminine scent, and then he'd cupped her face between his hands. "You can buck and kick all you like, Tori, but we aren't going to give up."

She huffed out an exasperated breath, stepped away, and turned her back to him. He'd stood there watching her for a while but when he noticed how tense her shoulders were, he'd given her some space and headed to the dining room.

He could see desire and the knowledge in her eyes every time she met one of their gazes, but she always looked away after a few seconds. But he had hope and he wasn't giving up. Whenever the three of them were nearby her cheeks always seemed to be flushed and her eyes literally sparkled with arousal. She also fidgeted in her seat and looked as tense as all get out. No, Tori Springer wasn't immune to him and his brothers, and if he—they—just bided their time, they would get their chance.

There was no way in hell he was allowing her to get away from him without seeing where the attraction between all four of them led. That just wasn't an option.

* * * *

Tori hadn't had any luck getting a job and decided she couldn't wait any longer and made the decision to start up her own business. She had been working her ass off all week and even though she was tired, she was also wired with excitement. She had spent day after day going into the businesses in Slick Rock and asking the owners about their experiences when they first started up their shops and offices, and she felt like she was ready for the next step.

Last night she had stayed up until the wee hours of the morning formulating a business plan and setting it out on paper. She'd gone to the real estate office and talked with Steven and Giles Blaze and had asked about shop space for lease. Lucky for her, they had just the building, and Steven had taken her to the empty building at the end of the main street, which was also across from the gas station. It was a prime location and had a large window front. If she was able to talk the bank manager into giving her a business loan she suspected that she would end up with a lot of customers because of the great position. The large building would need to be cleaned and fitted out, but Tori had never been afraid of hard work, much to her mother's and Frank's disgust.

Tori had been a little afraid when Frank had turned his temper on her after she'd refused his money, but she'd held her ground. When her mother had just stood nearby and looked at Tori as if she was disappointed with her, she hadn't really cared. But what hurt the most was that her mother hadn't told her how proud she was for being independent or encouraged her to go after her goals. Her mother had looked at her as if she were a stranger, the way she treated all the servants.

She didn't remember everything that had gone by before Frank came on the scene except for some snippets and pieces. But what she did remember she liked. Her mom used to sit with her on her lap and read to her while they cuddled, but when Frank came along that had gone by the wayside. Besides giving Felicity a hug when they'd met again after a few years apart, Tori couldn't remember the last time she had any physical human contact. No, that wasn't true.

She could still remember how it felt to be in Luther's arms when he carried her away from the dead snake more than a week ago, and she had been aware of every nuance of movement he made. The way his muscles rippled and moved as he carried her, and the heat that had emanated from his body had been astounding. It had been very hard to release her arms from around his neck and then to push off his lap. She'd felt safe and secure in his arms, and even though she was also turned on by him and his brothers, almost as if she belonged with them all, she couldn't let her guard down.

"Get them out of your head, Tori. They only want you because they lust after you. No one really gives a damn about you," she muttered as she stared at the bank building. She had made an appointment the day before and was due inside in ten minutes. After taking a deep breath she exhaled and then drew in another, trying to calm her raucous nerves. Her palms were sweaty and her heart rate was elevated with anxiety, but she needed to do this.

If it hadn't been for what Felicity said the other day she'd never have thought of it. She owed Flick big time and planned to take her friend out as a thank-you for everything she and her husbands had done for her. If it hadn't been for them she would never have had the gumption to be where she was today.

After taking another few calming breaths, Tori grabbed the folder with all her projections and plans in it and headed into the bank. She walked over to the reception area and smiled at the young auburn-haired woman.

"Hi, I'm Tori Springer and I have an appointment with Mr. Wendall at nine thirty."

"Take a seat, Ms. Springer. I'll let Mr. Wendall know you're here."

Tori turned, took a seat on the sofa across from the reception desk, and wiped her sweaty palms surreptitiously on her black skirt. She glanced around the small bank, noting that most of the tellers were elderly women, and she was glad that the small town didn't seem to discriminate because of age or gender. There was only one man, and he and the receptionist looked to be their youngest employees.

"Ms. Springer," the receptionist said. "If you'll follow me, Mr. Wendall is ready to see you now."

"Thank you." Tori followed and when the receptionist opened a door at the end of the hall, she quietly took another deep breath, made sure her spine was straight and her shoulders were back, and hoped like hell she was portraying a confidence she was far from feeling. She walked into the large office after the woman urged her in, and she took a step forward as the door behind her closed.

Tori was surprised to see the man behind the large desk was young, although older than her, but still he must have been good at his job to have made manager of the bank at such a young age. She hoped that was a plus because sometimes older men thought that women shouldn't work or own their own business. Just like Frank.

Pushing those distressing thoughts aside, Tori walked over to the desk as Mr. Wendall rose to his feet and came around to greet her. After shaking her hand he gestured toward one of the chairs in front of his desk and then walked back around to his own seat.

"What can I do for you, Ms. Springer?"

"I'd like to take out a business loan, Mr. Wendall."

The next hour passed more quickly than Tori had expected. She went over the plan she'd stayed up late doing the previous evening and answered all Mr. Wendall's questions. By the time she'd finished she was totally drained and hoped that her weariness didn't show on her face. The whole time she'd been talking Mr. Wendall's expression had remained stoic, and she had no idea if she had convinced him that she could make a go of her own business or not, but she was pleased with the way she had handled herself and had been able to answer every question he'd asked her.

"If I let you have this loan, when would you want it by?" Mr. Wendall leaned back in his chair, rested his elbows on his desk, and placed the fingertips of his hands together, sort of like he was praying, but not quite.

"I'd like to get it as soon as possible. That is if you're willing to give me the loan."

"Hmm, you know, I've been looking into some businesses myself to invest in. I really like your ideas, Ms. Springer. The plan you set out is clear and concise, and this town is certainly expanding rapidly." He lowered his hands and leaned forward slightly. "Do you know about the—unusual relationships in Slick Rock?"

"Yes, sir, I do. I'm currently staying with my friend Felicity on the Double E Ranch."

"Good. Then you've obviously realized that this town needs the shop you're planning to set up." Mr. Wendall pushed his chair back, rose to his feet, and walked around to the front of his desk. The man was tall, muscular, and handsome but he did nothing for her libido.

Wait! Does that mean he's going to give me the loan? Please? Please? Please God?

"I would love to be able to give you the hundred percent that you've asked for, but after the GFC and the slow recovery of the economy, that just isn't viable. Not good business, as I am sure you understand."

Disappointment coursed through her heart, but Tori hoped it didn't show on her face. She didn't move or speak because for some reason she didn't think Mr. Wendall had finished talking.

"But..." He held up a finger as if she might try to interrupt. "I would be willing to be a silent partner with you, if that is acceptable to you, Ms. Springer."

"You would?"

Mr. Wendall smiled and then he laughed. She must have looked as shocked as she felt. "Why don't I order some coffee for us and we can talk over everything?"

Tori just nodded and he reached for the phone on his desk and, after placing the order for coffee, sat down next to her to work. By the time she left his office three hours later her head was spinning, but she was buzzing with enthusiasm. She had opened a business account at the bank and Mr. Wendall had put his share of money into it. Then he'd approved the business loan from the bank and added the rest of the money. She felt like she was flying high and she wanted to race back to the ranch and tell Felicity about all her plans, but she needed to stop into the real estate office. She was going to be buying that large shop instead of leasing it like she'd first thought.

After dealing with Steven and Giles, signing the paperwork and handing over a deposit, Tori was so full of excitement she could barely contain it. The drive back to the ranch seemed to take forever but really only took her the usual twenty minutes. After parking her car and grabbing her paperwork and her purse, she hurried inside and went in search of Felicity.

Tori Springer was going to be part owner in her own business.

She found Felicity in the kitchen with her head in the fridge and when Felicity looked at her over her shoulder, she closed the door and turned to face her.

"Where have you been going all week? What are you up to, girl?"

Those two questions released the excitement bubbling up inside and she began explaining. Tori knew she was talking a mile a minute, but once she started speaking she had to get it all out. By the time she'd finished Felicity was laughing and hurried over to her and gave her a hug.

"You are unbelievable, Tori Springer. I can't believe you. You're so smart."

"I got the idea when you said you had to travel nearly two hours to go to a baby store. With all the ménage relationships in town and seeing that they have started families, it just made sense."

"You said that Trick Wendall is going to be a silent partner?" Felicity asked.

"Yes." Tori nodded and then went on to explain how they were going fifty-fifty with the business.

"You don't think he has a hidden agenda, do you?"

"What do you mean?"

"I can't believe how naïve you are at times, Tori. You're a very attractive woman. Men watch you all the time."

"They do not."

"See. I rest my case. You are totally oblivious except when it comes to the Katz brothers."

"What? No. No. No. No, damn it. Don't you dare try to match-make." Tori crossed her arms over her chest in a defensive move but also to hide her burgeoning nipples. Her body responded at the most inopportune of times. Especially when she thought of those three handsome, sexy men. Or when they were in the room with her. Or when she dreamed about them touching her at night. She sighed with resignation. She pretty much thought about them all the time and was in a constant state of arousal. Hopefully by the time she had the shop up and running she would have some money left over to lease her own place and she could put them out of her mind.

Yeah right. As if that is ever going to happen.

"There is nothing like that, Flick. We're only going to be business partners. That's it."

"I hope you're right. Trick Wendall and his two brothers have been looking for a woman to settle down with for a few years now. Just make sure they know the score. Okay? I'd hate for you to get into a situation you can't get out of."

She would just treat Mr. Wendall like any other business colleague, and if he looked like he wanted more from her she would set him straight from the get-go, but she didn't think any of that would be necessary. She hadn't gotten any of those vibes from him. Not like she did from the Katz brothers. Tori nodded and pushed those thoughts aside.

"Do you want to go out and celebrate with me?" Tori asked.

"I would really like to." Felicity bit her lip as she hesitated. "But..."

"I'm really tired and don't think I would be great company, but if you'd like I can call some of the other women I know and see if they're going out tonight. The hotel is always busy and I know Tyson would keep an eye on you."

"I don't need to be looked after, Flick. I've been taking care of myself since I was five years old."

Felicity sighed and looked sad. "I know. We had similar childhoods, just in different ways. I'm never going to treat my kids the way you and I were treated."

"You don't." Tori gave her a smile. "Carly Rose knows she's loved. She's such a happy little girl and the baby you've got in your womb is going to be just as cherished."

Flick sniffled and gave her a wobbly smile as she nodded her head. "Thank you. Damn these pregnancy hormones."

Tori wiped her moist eyes and then gave Felicity a hug. "God, we're a pair."

Felicity laughed. "That we are. Now what are we going to do about getting you out to celebrate? I don't like the thought of you being out on your own."

"We can take her."

Tori gave a soft squeal and spun around. Three tall, sexy men stood just inside the kitchen doorway and they were all looking at her. She'd had no idea they'd come into the room and hoped they hadn't been standing there all along. She and Felicity had talked about some things that were private to her and didn't want anyone else besides her closest friend knowing. But as she tried to read their expressions she became frustrated. The three Katz brothers were really good at hiding their emotions and what they were thinking, so she gave up and finally looked away.

She started to shake her head at their offer of taking her out, but Felicity stepped in front of her. "That's a great idea. I know you will make sure she's safe. In fact I think you should take her out to dinner, too. Tori has been doing all the cooking and cleaning as well as…other stuff and deserves a night off."

Tori started to edge away from Felicity and thanked God there was another exit on the dining room side of the room. She didn't want to go out with the Katz brothers because she had a feeling if she did, then her life would never be the same again and she wasn't sure that was a good thing, especially now that she was going to be starting her own business. She was going to need all her time getting things set up and didn't want anything or anyone standing in her way.

She kept her eyes on Luther but felt her cheeks heat with desire and embarrassment and lowered her gaze to the floor. Tori couldn't believe the way she was behaving. These men seemed to bring what she considered her worst traits to the fore, and she didn't like that.

For a time while she had been living with Frank and her mom in that great hulking mansion, she let them dictate to her and she'd become almost introverted. But when she'd finished high school and put herself through college she'd become independent and she liked being that way. She wasn't about to let these men take over and control her. She'd had enough of people controlling her life, trying to make her decisions for her, and she wasn't about to let anyone start that again. Especially when other people's decisions regarding *her* life could be downright distasteful and destructive.

Tori had overheard her mom and Frank talking one night and she'd been horrified to discover he was going to try and set her up with one of his so-called business friends. His intention had been to marry her off, which would give him an *in* into the sector of business he'd been trying to break into for years. She'd put a stop to that very quickly. Tori had packed her bags, snuck out in the middle of the night, and run. She had been lucky enough to be able to stay at a fellow waitress's house for a couple of nights, until she'd been able to find her own apartment. Thank God she'd been saving every penny she earned from her part-time work in that restaurant, because if she hadn't she may well have ended up on the street.

Tori gasped, pulled from her disturbing memories when she bumped into a big, hard, muscular body, and barely held in a moan of desire when warm, brawny arms wrapped around her waist and tugged her up against his large frame.

"Going somewhere, Tori?"

She looked up and up and up and connected with Jeremiah's blue-green gaze and gulped while she shook her head. There she went again, off inside herself because of the way they intimidated her. But she wasn't scared that the Katz brothers would hurt her. Deep down she knew they wouldn't. She was frightened of the way they made her feel, the way her body went haywire and responded to all of them. She'd never felt so in tune to one man before, let alone three, and wasn't sure how to handle it.

"Are you scared of us, honey?" Jeremiah frowned down at her and looked like he was holding his breath while he awaited her answer.

Tori decided it was high time she found that backbone she'd discovered the day she'd left Frank's house and looked him square in the eyes. "No."

"Then why don't you prove it, Tori?"

"How?" Tori asked, knowing she was being reeled in like a fish on a hook, but she couldn't seem to stop herself from taking the bait.

"Let us take you out."

A shiver wracked her spine as Jeremiah's deep voice washed over her and her skin goose bumped. But when she felt a presence beside her she gulped again and found herself agreeing so she could get away from them faster.

"Okay." She felt like she was sinking to the bottom of the pool and she couldn't breathe. Tori felt like she was drowning in their heat, their scents, and their masculinity.

"We'll give you half an hour to get changed and then we'll head out." Luther's breath brushed against the side of her neck and the sensitive skin of her ear, and even though she wanted to turn her head and look at him, she kept her gaze centered on Jeremiah's cotton-covered chest.

But when she felt a whisper of a touch against her arm as Bryant moved to her other side, she knew she was doomed. She was surrounded by them and she liked it. Her pussy was clenching and weeping juices onto her panties. Her breasts felt swollen and achy and her nipples were hard and throbbing.

Shit. I'm going down and I don't know what to do to stop it.

Chapter Four

Bryant sat in the back of his brother's truck and studied Tori. She hadn't said anything other than thank you after he'd helped her up into the backseat and now she was staring out the side window.

He was glad that he, Luther, and Jeremiah had entered the kitchen when they had because they'd heard everything Tori and Felicity had talked about. He'd wanted to ask her about her childhood but knew it was too early for that yet. He and his brothers needed to instill some trust in her before they could go prying into her life. He'd been wracking his brain trying to work out how to go about that, but hadn't come up with anything so far. Hopefully his brothers would have an idea or two.

When she'd told Flick about going into business with the local bank manager he'd been jealous as hell, but knew Tori had been sincere when she'd said that she only saw him as a colleague. He and his brothers were going to have to keep an eye out for this Trick Wendall. If he looked like he was honing in on their woman they would have to put a stop to that quick.

When Luther looked at him in the rearview mirror and raised his eyebrow, he shook his head to let him know that Tori still hadn't looked at him. If she kept up the silent treatment it was going to make for one hell of an uncomfortable night, but then Bryant figured if he couldn't get her talking then none of them would. Even though he wasn't a chatterbox or very sociable he was more talkative and laid-back than his brothers. It was up to him to break the ice and get the ball rolling.

Luther was quiet most of the time, but if he saw something he wanted he went for it hard, never deviating from his goals. He and Jeremiah could be just as indefatigable, but they were different in going about getting what they wanted. And one thing they were determinedly resolute about was getting Tori Springer into their lives. Giving up and losing her before they even had her wasn't an option.

"We grew up in Wichita, Kansas," Bryant said and held in a smile when Tori turned to look at him. He had her attention and now all he had to do was keep it. That wasn't going to be as easy as it sounded.

"Our parents didn't meet until they were in their forties and we were late babies. By the time Luther and Jeremiah hit their twenties the ranch was getting too much for our folks and they were thinking of selling up and traveling before they got any older. At least that's what Dad said.

"Luther and Jer joined the Marines and I followed a few years later. We weren't worried about leaving our parents alone on the ranch, because they had good reliable hands and Dad didn't have any need to do too much strenuous work.

"Mom and Dad ummed and ahhed over selling the ranch, but still ended up doing the traveling they wanted to. But they had such a good time exploring our country they decided to sell up and had all the paperwork signed for an estate agent to do just that. They had a fax and a laptop in their motor home and could deal with everything without coming back. But they wanted to be home and make sure the new owners adhered to the agreement of keeping the ranch hands on as promised and to thank their loyal employees, and just say good-bye to the home they'd had for more than thirty years." Bryant scrubbed a hand over his face and swallowed. It still choked him up to talk about his mom and dad. He missed them so damn much.

He opened eyes he hadn't been aware he'd closed when he felt a soft, feminine touch on his arm, and without thinking about what he was doing he clasped Tori's hand and laced his fingers with hers. She gave him a slight squeeze as if encouraging him to continue, so he took a deep breath and did just that.

"They never made it home. One of the tires on their motor home blew out. Dad must have lost control and the thing tipped over. They were traveling down a steep incline with sheer drops on either side of the road. The motor home tipped over the guard rail. Neither of them stood a chance."

"I'm sorry," Tori said, her voice cracking slightly, and when he looked up into her eyes he saw the tears on her eyelashes and more spilled over and down her face.

And that was the moment Bryant fell head-over-heels in love with her. He hated seeing her crying and needed her close. After unclipping her safety belt he gave her hand a gentle tug and he was pleased when she didn't resist. She scooted into the middle of the seat. He made sure she was clipped into the middle seat belt and then he wrapped an arm around her shoulders, pulling her up tight against his side. Tori leaned her cheek on his chest and cried quietly. Bryant had a feeling the tears she was shedding were due to so much more than telling her about when their parents had died.

Now that he seemed to have broken through to her heart, would she open up with them and accept being in a relationship with them?

He glanced into the rearview mirror at Luther and nodded his head. His brother would know what he wanted without having to tell him verbally. The truck slowed and then Luther pulled off into a parking area on the side of the road. Bryant was pleased that the trees would obscure the truck from any passing cars. He didn't want any interruptions while they talked with Tori and just hoped she would actually talk to them more from now on.

Luther turned off the ignition and he and Jeremiah got out of the truck. Bryant released both his and her seat belts, and after opening the door he scooped her up into his arms and got out. He carried her over to the timber table and bench seats and sat down with her on his lap.

She looked up at him with bloodshot eyes and a tear-streaked face, and she looked so beautiful and vulnerable his heart did a flip in his chest. This was the moment he and his brothers had been waiting for, and they had to tread very carefully with her. The last thing he wanted was for him and his brothers to screw this up.

"I'm sorry," Tori said, her voice breaking on a hiccup.

Luther and Jeremiah sat on the table on either side of them, their feet on the wooden bench seats, facing him and Tori.

"What's wrong, baby?" Luther asked in a soft voice.

Bryant was surprised by his big brother's tone. He'd never used that voice with anyone before, but he was glad his hard-ass brother was being cautious with her.

"I'm sorry you lost your parents. It's really hard to lose someone you love."

"You sound like you know from experience?" Bryant made his words into a question, hoping she would supply them with more information about her life.

She nodded. "My dad died when I was a little girl."

"Damn, honey, we're sorry, too." Jeremiah stroked her cheek and looked sad for Tori.

"How did your momma cope?" Luther asked, surprising Bryant again with his compassion. His big brother usually didn't give a shit about anyone else. This sensitivity proved to him that Tori was special to all of them, which he'd already known, but seeing Luther working hard to get into the depths of Tori's soul gave him more hope than he'd ever had that this could actually work out.

"She didn't." Tori sighed. "She cried a lot of course. We both did, but with each day she seemed to close herself off a little more."

She took a deep breath and exhaled slowly, as if trying to control her emotions. "Six months after my dad died she met Frank Stuttgart. The moment my mother started going out with him she changed even more."

"That doesn't sound good, darlin'." Bryant rubbed his hand up and down her back when he felt her tense up further. He hoped that his caresses gave her the courage to continue talking as he offered her the little comfort he could.

"No. Momma became much colder. She used to read to me all the time just before it was time for bed, but after Daddy died she stopped doing that. She used to hold me on her lap and cuddle with me, but after my father passed on and Frank came on the scene she kept me at an arm's length. She never hugged or kissed me again. Never told me how much she loved me like she used to do."

"Shit." Luther bent down, took her hand in his, and threaded their fingers together. "How old were you when your dad died, baby?"

"Five," she whispered.

Bryant's heart clenched with the pain that five-year-old Tori had suffered and knew that suffering had continued on throughout her childhood. She was still suffering and it hurt so much to see the sadness and dejection in her eyes. No wonder she'd kept trying to push them away.

He glanced at his brothers and saw that they were hurting for her, too. Tori Springer had been hurt so bad by her mother, she'd been too scared to get close to anyone ever since. Now that they understood why, hopefully they could show her just how special she was.

"Your stepfather and mother should be horsewhipped," Jeremiah said in an angry voice.

Tori looked up at him as if she was shocked by his statement and Bryant realized then that she had no one but herself to rely on. As far as he was concerned that was all about to change. He and his brothers wanted to be there for her. Bryant wanted her to let go of some of that control and lean on them. He knew it wouldn't happen overnight, but if they played their cards right they could have something really special with Tori.

Failing wasn't an option.

"That wasn't the worst of it." Tori's quiet voice broke the silence, but her words caused him and his brothers to tense up.

Jeremiah had one hand clenched into a fist and Luther was grinding his teeth. Bryant's thigh muscles flexed and he had to consciously concentrate on relaxing them and hoped that Tori hadn't felt the change in him. He didn't want her to feel his emotional turmoil right now. He wanted her to keep talking.

"What was worse, darlin'?" Bryant asked the question they were all waiting to hear the answer to.

"Frank was going to try and marry me off to one of his business colleagues to get into a sector of business he'd been trying to break into for years."

Bryant suppressed his roar of fury, barely, and from the look of horror on his brothers' faces they were doing the same.

"Fuck!" Jeremiah's knuckles cracked from clenching his fist so hard.

"I heard my mother and Frank talking one night. I was thirsty and was heading to the kitchen to get a drink of water, but my mom and Frank were already in there. The door was slightly ajar and I stopped when I heard my name mentioned." Tori paused and swallowed audibly before taking a deep breath to continue. "They planned to take me out for dinner, but they were going to haul me in front of a justice of the peace and try and make me marry a man I'd never even met."

"Fucking hell." Luther released Tori's hand, jumped off the table and began to pace back and forth.

"How old were you, honey?" Jeremiah's voice was tight with anger.

"Eighteen."

"Jeezus," Bryant whispered, scared he would upset her if he spoke any louder, but it had been really hard to keep his voice so soft. He was raging inside and had to swallow several times before he was able to even think he'd be able to speak.

"What did you do?" Jeremiah asked in a raspy voice, beating Bryant to the question he'd been about to ask.

"I packed a bag, waited until I was sure they were asleep, and left."

"Where did you go?" Luther asked after he sat down next to them on the bench.

"I'd been working part time in a restaurant after school, on the weekends and during the holidays. I went to one of the other waitress's home and stayed there for a couple of nights."

"Only a couple—" Bryant began to ask but she cut him off.

"Frank was horrified when I got a job and tried to get me to quit, but I stood my ground. I'd been saving every penny I could since I intended to leave once I started college anyway. He didn't want me boarding at college and wanted to give me an allowance, but I refused to take his money. I swear that man was born in the eighteenth century. He thought that a woman's place was in the home and only allowed out when he wanted someone to decorate his arm or make him look good to his business colleagues. But that's not me."

Tori sighed. "I roomed at college, and after I got my degree rented a small one-bedroom apartment. It took a year before my mother contacted me to see if I was still alive and all right, I guess, and even though I've seen her a couple of times, she and Frank keep trying to run my life. She called me this morning and wanted me to drop everything to go back home to look after the great ugly museum they call a house, but I refused. There's no need since they have a contingency of servants who live on the property.

"My mom told me I was a disappointment to her and that I was no longer her daughter." She finished the last sentence on a sob and Bryant couldn't stand seeing the pain in her eyes. He wrapped his arms around her and held her tight while she cried. He hated to see her so upset but there was nothing he could do about her mother and stepfather. But from now on he and his brothers would show her how much they cared and hopefully she would begin to care for them, too.

When she'd finished crying she sat up straighter, wiped the moisture from her cheeks and eyes, and drew in a shuddering breath. Luther pulled a clean handkerchief from his pocket and handed it to her.

"Tori, I don't condone what your mother has done to you, but I think the death of your father hurt her badly and it looks to me like she's never really recovered from her grief." Luther cupped her cheek in his hand and stared into her red-rimmed eyes. Bryant was pleased to see that Tori didn't try to pull away or break their visual connection. That had to be a good thing, didn't it? "I think the only way for your mother to cope with the loss of the love of her life was to close herself off from everything and everyone."

"That makes sense," Jeremiah said. "Maybe Frank's coldness was what she needed to continue on living. You were so young and from what I've gathered you mother didn't have anyone to turn to."

Tori frowned and then nodded her head. "Both my parents were only children. Dad's parents were killed just after Mom and Dad got married, in some sort of accident. I never met my mother's father. He died before I was even born and so did my mom's mother. I remember snippets of conversations my parents had, but I was just a little kid and didn't feel I could ask Mom anything after she closed herself off."

I know it's hard, darlin'," Bryant said. "Especially after what you've been through, but you need to try and forgive your mom, even if you never see her again. Don't hold a grudge against her. It will only tear you up inside."

Tori nodded and then she surprised the hell out of him. She wrapped her arms around his waist and nuzzled his chest with her cheek. "Thank you." She reached up and kissed him on the cheek, sat up straight again, and then took one of Jeremiah's and Luther's hands into her own. "Thanks, all of you, for listening to me. I'm not normally so emotional."

"Don't apologize for feeling, baby. We're just glad that you took the time to talk to us." Luther leaned forward and placed a light kiss on her lips. Bryant had to hold in his excitement when he noticed her body's response.

Tori's pupils dilated and she began to lightly pant. When Luther moved back, Jeremiah slid from the table, sat on their other side of the bench, and lightly tugged on her ponytail. She turned toward him and held her breath when Jeremiah gave her a soft kiss on the lips, too. His brothers stood up and started back toward the truck, and Bryant stood up, taking her with him. He heard her exhale in a whoosh and then he, too, kissed her soft, delectable mouth.

What he really wanted to do was ravish her until she was whimpering with need, but Tori wasn't ready for that just yet. If he had his way she would be very, very soon.

Chapter Five

Tori couldn't believe how easy it had been to talk to Luther, Jeremiah, and Bryant. The only other person she had told her secrets to had been Felicity. But after the phone call from her mother a week ago and then hearing about the death of their parents, she'd fallen apart. She'd never done that before either.

What was it about the Katz brothers that got to her in so many ways? Besides the physical attraction, they now had her spilling her guts about her life story. Not that it really mattered one way or another. It wasn't like she was giving away state or country secrets. But she'd never felt this way before. Now that she'd opened up with them, so to speak, she felt a whole lot better. The pain that had been festering inside her had gone and now she only felt pity for her mother. Maybe one day her mom would wake up and want a real mother-daughter relationship, but she wouldn't hold her breath.

Tori was surrounded by their heat and she had been in a constant state of arousal from the first day she'd met the Katz brothers. It was really hard to keep her attraction at bay when what she really wanted to do was kiss and touch them all over.

A little piece of the ice that had encased her heart had melted as they'd listened to her talk, cursed when they got angry on her behalf, and soothed her when she cried. She was currently holding hands with Bryant and Jeremiah as they led her to a table in the Slick Rock Hotel, and she could feel the heat emanating from Luther as he walked close behind her.

Another shiver ran up and down her spine when he placed his hand on her shoulder, and she had the urge to look back at him over her shoulder but was worried if she did she would trip or something. Every time she looked at these three men her heart raced and her pussy got wet. She wasn't sure how much more she could stand.

After Jeremiah and Bryant seated her and the three men sat down, too, the waitress handed out the menus and took their drink orders. Tori was ravenous after crying and felt so much lighter after sharing her problems, so instead of ordering her usual salad she ordered a steak, baked potato, and salad.

Luther and Bryant were sitting across the table from her and Jeremiah was right next to her. After their drinks were served Luther leaned forward and Tori did the same, curious about what he wanted to say.

"We want to have a relationship with you, Tori. We're very attracted to you."

"I'm not sure—"

Jeremiah placed his hand over the one she had resting on the table. "What are you afraid of, honey?"

Tori gulped and shook her head, not sure how to put what she was thinking into words.

"Talk to us, Tori," Luther commanded with implacability and she found herself complying with his will.

"I'm not sure I can handle more than one man," she said quietly, aware of the other diners around them and not wanting strangers to hear a private conversation.

Bryant must have seen her glancing around them and realized she was uncomfortable with the subject and setting. "We can talk about this later." He stared at both his brothers and then smiled at her. "Tonight is for relaxing and having a good time."

Tori nodded and sighed with relief. Bryant seemed to be very in tune with her and that just made her like him even more. For such a big, brawny man to know how she was feeling was nice and made her feel warm and fuzzy inside. He was taking care of her and they weren't even going out.

They began asking her about her plans for her new business and they listened as she explained what she wanted and even gave her a few suggestions she took on board. Their dinner was served and she asked them whether they'd found a place they wanted to buy since they wanted their own ranch.

"We have a couple of prospects we plan to look at on Monday," Luther said and then he and his brothers told her they wanted organic-fed beef and how they intended to grow their own pesticide-free crops. By the time they'd finished eating Tori felt really relaxed and comfortable with them.

She looked up when someone called her name.

"Hi, Tori, I thought that was you. How are you, partner?"

"Trick, hi. I'd like you to meet Luther, Jeremiah, and Bryant Katz."

Trick shook hands with all three men and Tori had to bite her tongue when Jeremiah placed his arm over her shoulder in a show of possessiveness. The rat looked pleased when Trick followed the move and then looked at all three men and her with speculation in his eyes. She knew he was going to grill her when she met him at the shop on Monday morning.

"Are you here alone? Would you like to join us?" Tori turned to glare at Luther when she heard him make a growly noise before turning back to face Trick.

"No thanks, Tori. I'm with my brothers. Make sure you stopover before you leave so I can introduce you." Trick smiled at her and then headed across the other side of the room. She followed him with her eyes to see his brothers sitting at a table eating their just-delivered meals.

"What the hell was that?" Tori asked as she stared at Luther.

He looked away while clearing his throat and then met her gaze again, looking a bit chagrined. "Sorry, I didn't do it on purpose. It just sort of happened. Kind of like animal instinct or something."

Tori turned to Jeremiah and shrugged her shoulders to displace his arm. "And don't think I don't know what you were doing either. I'm not even going out with you and you're both behaving like cavemen. If—and that's a big if, because I haven't made up my mind yet—if I do go out with you, all of that will stop. I won't put up with you three trying to control me or get caught in the middle of a pissing contest. Do I make myself clear?"

"Yes, ma'am. Sorry, honey." Jeremiah leaned over and kissed her cheek.

"I'm sorry, too, baby." Luther scrubbed a hand over his face.

"Apology accepted. Just don't do it again."

"No, ma'am."

Bryant burst out laughing and it was really hard to keep a straight face. His eyes sparkled and his whole face lit up with his humor.

"What's so damn funny?" Luther scowled at him.

"You two are." Bryant met her gaze and smiled. "You're one hell of a woman, darlin'. I love that you stood up to these two Neanderthals."

Tori smiled and when Bryant got up from his chair and walked around to her she wondered what he was doing.

"Dance with me, darlin'?" he asked and held his hand out to her.

She clasped his hand and he helped her to her feet, leading the way to the dance floor. Instead of placing a hand on her hip and holding her hand at chest height like she expected, Bryant pulled her up close against his body so that the entire length of her, from breasts to knees, was touching him.

She gulped when her pussy clenched, her clit throbbed, and cream dripped onto her panties. Her breasts felt fuller and her nipples were pushing against her bra and shirt. She hoped that he couldn't feel them poking into his chest.

The song had a fast beat, but that didn't seem to bother Bryant. He just swayed to the music as if a slow song was playing. She wanted to rest her head on his chest and wrap her arms around his waist, but she didn't want to make a spectacle of herself when there were other people around.

"What has you worried about being with all of us, Tori?"

She shivered when his warm breath caressed her ear and then she looked up at him and felt like she was drowning in his eyes. The pull was magnetic, and no matter how hard she tried, she couldn't break it. But then she realized she didn't really want to and that worried her a little.

"I don't know if one woman is enough for three men and I don't want to lose any part of myself."

Bryant sighed and then his hand slid from her waist until it was lower down her back and at the top of her ass.

"How can you think that, darlin'? You've seen the way Felicity and her husbands are. They are all very happy people and you can see how much they love each other."

"I'm not Felicity."

"No, you're not. You are a beautiful, sexy, strong-minded, smart woman. We wouldn't take you over, Tori. Yes, my brothers can be arrogant asses as you've already seen, and I can be, too, but you stood right up to them and by doing so you earned their respect. Didn't you see the pride in Luther's eyes when you shot him down? We knew you weren't a pushover by the way you kept away from us, but you just confirmed that you have what it takes to stand up for yourself and not be pushed around. Although why he had to test you after the way you dealt with your mom and stepfather is beyond me."

"He was testing me?" Tori frowned at him.

"Yes, but Luther didn't really think about it consciously. Both he and Jeremiah were being arrogant assholes and staking a claim on you in front of your new partner. He was making sure that Trick knew you were taken."

"I figured that one out. But why? He—none of you have a claim on me."

"But we want to." Bryant's voice was full of sincerity and hope, but she couldn't give him what he wanted. At least not yet. Tori needed more time to get to know them better before making such a big decision. She'd only had two boyfriends and both those men had turned out to be real assholes. She'd learned to be cautious.

Plus she was more than a little worried that she couldn't satisfy one man let alone three. She'd never even had an orgasm before, at least not while awake, and her last boyfriend had told her it was her fault that he'd strayed because she wasn't woman enough to satisfy him. That had been one of the reasons she had decided to avoid romantic entanglements with the opposite sex.

And then there was the fact she was about to start her own business. She wasn't going to have much spare time, and if she did begin a relationship with the Katz brothers, would they feel neglected because she was so busy? Also they were going to be running their own ranch soon and that would be even less time they got to spend together.

Tori just couldn't see it working out and wondered if it was even worthwhile thinking about it. But the thought of walking away and never finding out what could be hurt more than she expected it to.

Before she agreed to what they wanted they were all going to have to sit down and talk about it. She wouldn't have them whining and bitching at her because she spent too much time at work, and she didn't want to end up nagging them for the same reason.

There was going to have to be a lot compromise from all of them and also understanding. She wasn't sure Luther would be considerate if she was tired and wanted to spend some time alone. She'd been on her own for so long, she knew she would need some time out now and then and could just imagine him and Jeremiah getting pissed at her if she didn't spend enough time with them.

"Stop overthinking things, Tori. We can talk more, later." Bryant slowly turned her in a circle. "Just relax and enjoy the night."

When the song ended Bryant led her back to the table, but she didn't get to sit down. Luther stood up and clasped her hand. "Would you dance with me?"

Tori nodded and tried to hold the shiver in that worked its way up her spine but knew she hadn't been successful when Luther gave her a heated look. He guided her back to the dance floor and took her into his arms.

"I'm sorry I was such an ass before. I don't mean to be an arrogant prick, but I can't stand the way other men look at you."

"There is nothing between Trick Wendall and me, Luther. I'm not some whore that jumps into bed with just anyone."

"God, Tori, that's not what I meant. I'm—*we're* really attracted to you, and the thought of you going out with someone else ties me in knots."

"That's not going to happen," Tori said and then nearly moaned out loud when she inhaled his intoxicating manly scent. He smelled so good. Clean, fresh male mixed in with a slight woodsy fragrance. She couldn't get enough of any of their scents, and even though she knew she just may well end up going crazy with unrequited lust, she couldn't seem to help herself.

She looked up into his eyes and again found it hard to break the visual connection. Why did she have to be attracted to three men now? Just when it looked like she was going to be able to get her life back on track. At least where her career was concerned.

"Are you intimidated by the thought of being with three men?" Luther asked and then he cursed. "Shit. I didn't mean to blurt that out. That makes me sound egotistically arrogant."

His back step made her realize he wasn't sure about her at all and that made the ice casing around her heart melt a little more.

"I know what you meant, Luther."

"Thank God for that," he muttered and she nearly laughed because she didn't think she was supposed to hear that. He must have seen the humor in her eyes because the corners of his mouth lifted slightly and his eyes crinkled.

"You're so beautiful, Tori." He leaned down and brushed his lips against her temple. "Is Tori short for something? Victoria maybe?"

"No. It's just Tori."

"Short and sweet, just like you," Luther said with such sincerity her chest filled with warmth and her eyes burned with unshed tears. She fell for him even more in that instant and knew there was no way in hell she could walk away from the three Katz brothers without finding out if they could have something worth holding onto.

"Sweet, pfft. But I'm not short, just vertically challenged. Besides, you three are hunky, muscular giants compared to me." Tori looked up when Luther didn't say anything and then she watched with lust and awe as a slow smile spread across his face. It took her a moment or two to realize what she'd said and she lowered her gaze as her cheeks heated.

"You're not used to getting compliments, are you, baby?" Luther murmured near her ear, and Tori shook her head slightly, glad he didn't say anything about her calling them hunky. "You'll be getting a lot more of them from now on, Tori."

Tori didn't say anything. She couldn't. She was too overcome with emotion and she decided that she didn't really need to reply anyway. Instead she just relished being in Luther's arms and having his big hard body pressed against hers. Usually if she felt a hard cock against her while she was dancing she would have been repulsed, but she didn't feel one bit revolted by having his erection pressing into her stomach and she hadn't when she'd felt Bryant's cock either.

The song ended and Luther wrapped an arm around her waist and led her back to the table. After retaking her seat she took a sip of the fresh, cool wine and listened as the three Katz brothers talked about the properties they were going to view on Monday. They were so enthusiastic about running and owning their own ranch again that Tori got caught up in their excitement and found herself smiling and laughing with them. She felt so carefree and hadn't felt that way since she was five years old. She liked it.

Jeremiah tapped her arm to get her attention and when she turned to face him she felt her face heat at the hunger she saw in his blue-green eyes. "Would you dance with me, Tori?"

"Yes."

He helped her to her feet and she held his hand as he led her to the dance floor. When he took her into his arms she sighed with contentment.

"Are you okay, honey?"

"Yeah, I'm fine."

"When was the last time you had a night out?"

"It's been a while," Tori hedged while she tried to remember the last time she'd been on a date. It had been over two years, but she didn't mind. She'd been busy with college and then trying to map out a career for herself in the travel industry, which had turned out to be a waste of time.

"What are you thinking about?" Jeremiah asked as he rubbed his whiskered chin against the top of her head, which caused goose bumps to race across her skin.

"About the time I wasted in my last job."

"I don't think it was a waste."

Tori leaned back to look up at him and yet again found herself entranced in the hypnotic pull of one of the Katz brother's eyes.

"You don't?"

"No." Jeremiah drew her back into his arms.

"You learned how to deal with the public and soothe snobby egos. I think you'll find that experience invaluable when you have your business up and running."

Tori hadn't thought about it like that and realized that Jeremiah was right.

"Hmm, you have me there." She sighed and snuggled up against him, aware of the hard ridge against her stomach.

These three men made her feel soft like she imagined a woman wanted to feel, and she wanted to hold onto that sensation for as long as she could. It made her feel feminine to know that she could arouse these three confident, older, sophisticated men just by dancing with them, and she hadn't felt that way...ever.

Chapter Six

Jeremiah was so hard he was aching. Holding Tori in his arms felt so right. It was like everything he'd been searching for clicked into place. He loved the little sighing sounds she made and knew she wasn't even aware she was making them. Tori Springer felt like longevity, love, and warmth, as well as home and hearth all rolled into one.

He'd hated the way Trick Wendall looked at her earlier in the evening, and he didn't want her stopping to meet his brothers either. Jeremiah was jealous as hell, even if there hadn't been lust or interest in Trick's eyes. He hated anyone looking at the woman he considered his and his brothers'. Jeremiah knew he was being unreasonable, but Tori just seemed to bring out the animal in him as well as Luther. But he felt closer to her now than he had over the last couple of weeks. He was just glad that she'd finally opened up with them and told them about her life and worries. He wanted to be able to spend the rest of his life sharing in all the ups and downs, but mostly he wanted to spend his time loving her.

Tori hadn't had much love in her life, and with his brothers' help, hopefully they would be able to change that. Bryant was already well and truly in love with her. Jeremiah could see it every time he looked into his brother's eyes. He just hoped that Tori remained oblivious to his brother's emotions. The last thing he wanted was for her to step back because she was scared.

Jeremiah sighed with reluctance and eased his hold on her as the song ended and guided Tori back to their table. She sat down and took a couple of sips of her wine and then covered her mouth when she yawned. It was time to leave so she could get some rest. Tori was going to be flat-out busy as she and Trick got their shop ready to open up to the public.

"Are you ready to go, baby?" Luther asked.

"Yes." Tori smiled and then smothered another yawn. She looked them each in the eye before speaking again. "Thank you all so much for a wonderful night. I had a great time and it was just what I needed."

Jeremiah agreed with that last statement but didn't say so. Tori looked more relaxed than he'd ever seen her and he hoped that she stayed that way, but he didn't think that was likely to happen. Not when she had so much to do.

Jer helped her to her feet and kept her hand in his as he led her to the door but stopped and looked over his shoulder when she tugged back.

"Just a minute. I promised Trick that I would stop by to meet his brothers."

Jer cursed under his breath but followed her as she walked to the other side of the room.

Trick stood up when he saw her coming and then his brothers did, too, but when Trick took her free hand in his Jer wanted to knock him away. It took every bit of control he had to keep from doing that and from the smirk and gleam in Trick's eyes he knew how he felt.

"Tori, these are my brothers, Trent and Tristan."

"Hi," Tori said shyly, but when both Trent and Tristan offered their hands she shook them before withdrawing and moving closer to Jeremiah.

Jer looked down at her to see her blushing as the three Wendall brothers looked her over, and she moved closer again when Tristan smiled and winked at her.

"So you and Trick are going to be business partners?" Trent asked, and Tori nodded.

"We were just heading out," Tori said. "It was nice meeting you."

"The pleasure was all ours, Tori." Trent smiled. "We'll look forward to seeing more of you."

Tori blushed even more and then glanced at Trick. "I'll see you on Monday."

"That you will, sweetheart."

Jer glared at the Wendalls and had to stop himself from punching Trick in the face when he smiled.

Tori yanked his hand as she started walking to the exit again, and when they got outside he saw Bryant and Luther leaning against the truck.

"What's the holdup?" Luther scowled at Jer.

"Oh, sorry, I just went to meet Trick's brothers."

"What?" Luther snapped. "Why would you want to do that?"

"Because he asked me to." Tori pulled her hand from Jer's, turned to face Luther more fully, placed her hands on her hips, and frowned at him. "Do you have a problem with that?"

Jer knew that Tori speaking to Luther that way was like waving a red flag in front of a bull and hoped his arrogant brother didn't push her too far and send her running in the opposite direction. Especially when she was just warming up to them.

"Yeah, I do." Luther grabbed her hand and tugged so that she fell into him. He gripped her chin between his thumb and index finger, and then he was kissing her.

At first Tori was tense, but as the kiss deepened she melted into Luther's arms until her body was pressed against his. The kiss was long, deep, and wild and Jeremiah knew that Luther was losing control. His brother's hands were roaming all over Tori's body and she was moaning with desire.

Jer moved into Tori's back and pushed his hard cock into her back while tapping Luther on the shoulder. Luther slowed the kiss and finally lifted his head. His brother's face was flushed with arousal and his eyes hazed over with passion. He'd never seen Luther that turned on or so in tune with a woman before.

"It's time we left," Jeremiah said as he wrapped his arm around Tori's waist. Luther stepped back and he pulled her tighter into his body.

Bryant moved to stand in front of Tori and brushed a few strands of loose hair back from her face. "You okay, darlin'?"

Jer heard Tori gulp audibly and then she nodded.

"Come on, honey, let's get you into the truck." Jeremiah shoved Bryant out of the way, guided Tori to the back door, and after opening it, helped her up into the backseat. He followed her in. It was his turn to sit in the back with her since Bryant had traveled in the back with her on the way to the hotel.

When she went to scoot across to the far side, Jeremiah clasped her wrist and shook his head. She looked at him over her shoulder.

"Sit right here next to me, honey." He was pleased when she didn't protest and reached for the safety belt. After he helped buckle her in he wrapped his arm around her shoulders and drew her into his side.

She looked up at him with confusion in her eyes, but underlying that perplexity was desire and he couldn't hold back any longer. He turned to face her, gripped her ponytail gently but firmly, and then lowered his mouth to hers.

Jer groaned at his first taste of her and knew he wouldn't ever get enough of Tori Springer. He was aware he was doing just what Luther had done, but he couldn't seem to help himself. Jeremiah wanted her and he wanted her now.

She moaned as she leaned into him and when her hand came up to rest on his chest he felt elated. But when her hand slipped through the gap between his buttons his arousal shot into the heavens. Tori was touching him back and that was a very good thing. He wanted to do the same thing to her and push his hand under her shirt and mold her breasts with his hands and then he wanted to suck her hard little nipples into his mouth, but he didn't. Before this got any more out of hand he had to make sure that she was on board with all of them. Because once he and his brothers made love to her he was going to make sure that she knew damn well that there would be no turning back. She would belong to him, Luther, and Bryant from then on.

He eased the kiss down and looked at her passion-swollen lips and desire-hazed eyes as he tried to get his breathing back under control. Tori was panting more heavily than he was and that pleased him to no end.

"Tori, my brothers and I want to make love with you. We're very attracted to you, honey. When we get back to the bunkhouse will you let us pleasure you?"

She nibbled on her lip as she looked at him and he held his breath. She exhaled gustily and lowered her eyes to his crotch. He wanted to open his jeans and lower his zipper to ease the tight fit of his jeans, but he was a big man and he didn't want to frighten her with his voracious hunger.

He glanced toward the front and saw that Bryant had shifted in his seat so he could look into the back without straining his neck, and Luther kept glancing from the road to the rearview mirror and back again.

"Yes," Tori finally whispered her answer and he smiled so his brothers knew what her answer had been. He wasn't sure they'd heard her quiet reply.

Bryant grinned with what looked like jubilation and when he looked at Luther he knew his older brother was just as excited and relieved that she had accepted them. Luther's tension eased and his mouth was no longer held in a tight line and his brow had smoothed out from his frown.

Jeremiah wanted to kiss Tori again, but he knew if he started again he wouldn't stop, so he pulled her back into his arms and rested his chin on top of her head and just savored having her in his arms. It didn't matter that his cock was so hard it was aching and leaking pre-cum, or that his balls were throbbing as cum roiled around in them. All the mattered was having Tori in his arms. He inhaled deeply and shifted when he got of whiff of her strawberry scent and musky arousal. He wanted to strip her naked, lay her down on the backseat, and sink his cock balls-deep into her, but she deserved so much better than a quick fuck in the back of the truck.

It felt like forever before Luther pulled the truck up close to their bunkhouse, and Jeremiah was glad that their quarters were far enough away from the other bunkhouse where the regular hands were staying.

He didn't want to have to keep Tori quiet when they made her come. He wanted her to be so pleasured that she screamed their names when she climaxed.

Luther and Bryant were out of the truck before he could release his and Tori's safety belt. He hoped she wasn't put off or scared by his brothers' eagerness, but when she looked up at him as he got out, she smiled shyly at him.

He, Luther, and Bryant needed to take things slow with her. She still looked a little uncertain, and he hoped they could wipe that uncertainty from her mind. Jer lifted her from the truck, but instead of putting her down he nudged the door closed with his shoulder and then carried her inside.

* * * *

Tori clung to Jeremiah's neck as he carried her into the bunkhouse and tried to calm the rapid pace of her heart and her panting breaths. She looked around curiously and saw a large sofa in the living room area facing a large flat-screen TV on the far wall. There was even a hall, which she suspected led to the bathroom and bedrooms, and another door to the right led to a kitchen, which she doubted got much use except first thing in the morning, since the Katz brothers ate lunch and dinner at the main ranch house with Felicity and her husbands.

Jeremiah stopped in the middle of the room and she glanced at him and then to Bryant and Luther when they moved closer. Bryant smiled down at her and she could see the hunger in his blue eyes, but she was distracted by the dimples at the sides of his mouth. He had such a great smile and she was glad she got to see it often, but he also seemed to be very in tune to her feelings.

She looked at Luther to find him watching her avidly. He intimidated her a bit because of his big, tall, muscular physique and with his serious, intense personality, but she was also turned on by it. And then there was Jeremiah. He could be just as intense as Luther, but he could also joke around like Bryant. He was a mixture of his two brothers' personalities, but what worried her the most was how fast she was falling for all three of them. She knew that they wanted her, but what she didn't know was for how long.

Could she be setting herself up to get hurt, again?

One thing she was sure of was that she couldn't walk away from them. No one man had affected her this way let alone three. She needed to be with them. It was a compulsion, a hunger, a yearning she just couldn't ignore anymore. She needed them so damn much.

Luther palmed her cheek and stared into her eyes. "Make damn sure this is what you want, baby. Once we make love to you, you will belong to us. Do you understand?"

Tori nodded and wanted to ask how long they wanted her for, but bit her tongue. She didn't want to come across as too needy, too clingy, and turn them off. The men she'd met hated women to be clinging vines. Not that she was anything like that, especially after her childhood, but she didn't want to do anything to make them turn away from her.

"I need the words, Tori," Luther demanded.

"Yes," Tori whispered and continued when Luther quirked his eyebrow at her. "I understand."

"Take her to my room," Luther commanded and Jeremiah followed the directive.

Tori glanced into the two other bedrooms as Jeremiah carried her down the hall and when she saw the messy room she looked back over her shoulder to meet Bryant's eyes.

"Yours?"

Bryant grinned and nodded, not seeming to care that she'd seen his mess. She was glad because that meant he didn't conform to others' wishes like her mother had. Jeremiah's room was as neat as a pin and so was Luther's. She'd seen a couple of things on top of the dresser and bedside table as they passed Jeremiah's room, but Luther's room was sparsely furnished and absolutely nothing was out of place. And then she realized that Luther was a perfectionist and the leader of the three Katz brothers.

Tori had a feeling that she and Luther were going to clash because she had learned to be just the same way as him. It was the only way she felt she had control of her life, so she understood where Luther was coming from. She just hoped he didn't piss her off too much, or she him.

Jeremiah lowered her feet to the floor and held her waist until she was steady on her feet. Luther was leaning against the wall near the door with his bulging muscular arms crossed over his broad, brawny chest. Jeremiah moved to stand behind her and Bryant was standing in front of her but just to the right.

"Take your clothes off, Tori," Luther said in a quiet but commanding voice.

Tori shifted nervously from one foot to the other. She'd never undressed in front of a man while he watched her before. She'd only had sex twice, but each time her clothes had come off she'd been kissing her partner and the nudity had just been a natural flow and progression. This was different. There were three men with her and they were watching her expectantly.

"I…"

"Now, Tori."

"Luther…" Bryant started to speak and he had a frown on his face as he stared at his brother.

Tori didn't want them to fight because of her, so she lifted trembling hands to the buttons on her shirt and started undoing them. Bryant didn't say another word but watched as she opened each button. Excitement and nervousness warred in her belly causing her insides to quiver. She met Luther's eyes briefly but she looked away before she could figure out what the look in his gaze meant. Warmth raced through her veins and tingles raced over her skin, causing the fine hairs on her body to stand on end and goose bumps popped up all over.

Her nipples hardened even more and they began to throb in time with the beat of her heart. Jeremiah shifted on his feet drawing her attention and his eyes were glued to her fingers as she popped each button, but he was licking his lips as if they were dry. The muscles in his upper arms flexed and bulged and she looked down to see him gripping his thighs with his hands.

Is he trying to stop himself from touching me? She hesitated a moment and he smiled softly at her and nodded in encouragement.

Bryant looked like he had ants in his pants. He shifted from foot to foot constantly and when she followed the path of his hand she saw him adjusting his hard cock in his jeans. A nervous giggle formed in her chest and she was able to stop it from coming out of her mouth just in time. But when Bryant once more pulled at his jeans she moaned softly with desire.

She wanted to see what his cock looked like. She wanted to see all of them naked. Tori wanted to touch, kiss, and lick them all over, but most of all she wanted them filling her, loving her, and taking the incessant ache away.

With each button she released, her confidence grew, and the way they were all looking at her made her feel sexy. By the time she got to the last one she was panting and her pussy was dripping. Even though she was a little disconcerted, she was also hugely turned on and couldn't wait for them to kiss and touch her. Her legs were trembling and it was really hard to stand still. Her whole body felt weak and yet she also felt totally energized. There was a yearning throb deep inside her, which had been building from the moment she had first laid eyes on these three men. She was so hungry and horny she could barely think straight, but there was emotion involved, too. Tori could already feel all three of them in her heart, mind, and soul. She wanted this more than she'd ever wanted anything in her life. It didn't really matter that she was nervous. She hadn't even realized it but she had been waiting for this very moment the first time she'd seen all three of them leaning against the bar in the Slick Rock Hotel.

She shrugged her shoulders and the shirt fell off and down her arms to pool on the floor. She fumbled with the button on her jeans with trembling fingers but finally managed to flick it open, and then she lowered the zipper. After kicking off her slip-on shoes she slowly pushed her jeans over her hips and down her legs, and then stepped out of them.

"Beautiful," Bryant whispered as if trying not to break the tension in the room.

"Take off the rest, Tori," Luther demanded in a husky voice.

When she met his gaze she saw the famishment in his green eyes and realized he wasn't unaffected at all. She perused the length of his body and paused at his crotch when she saw the massive bulge beneath his jeans. Seeing the lust in his eyes as he stared at her gave her the confidence she needed to continue, and the next thing she knew she was standing before them totally naked.

"Damn," Luther rasped as he unfolded his arms. He pushed off the wall and walked toward her.

"You're a goddess, honey," Jeremiah said in hoarse voice.

Bryant stroked a hand from her shoulder down her arm and then he wrapped his arm around her waist. He pulled her up against his body, and groaned just before he slammed his mouth down onto hers.

Tori mewled with pleasure when he pushed his tongue into her mouth and twirled it around hers. She moaned when his other hand landed on her belly right above her hairless mound and caressed her.

"My turn," Luther said, and without any warning she was yanked out of Bryant's arms and lifted from her feet.

Tori draped her arms around Luther's neck and looked up just as his head was descending. His lips parted over hers and then he was kissing her voraciously. Her back landed on the bed, but she kept her eyes closed as Luther ravished her mouth. His big body came down on top of hers, his denim-covered legs brushing against her smooth ones and his cotton-covered chest rubbing across her nipples, making them ache even more, but he kept most of his weight off of her so he wouldn't crush her.

By the time Luther lifted his head, she was so breathless she couldn't drag enough air into her lungs, and cream was dripping from her pussy onto her inner thighs and down to coat her anus.

"Fucking perfect." Luther growled right before he shifted and then he sucked one of her nipples into his mouth.

She cried out at the exquisite, intense zings of pleasure that raced down her body and centered at her clit. The bed dipped on either side of her and she knew that Jeremiah and Bryant were next to her. She lifted passion-heavy eyelids and stared at them with awe for a moment. They were both naked and her pussy clenched, causing another gush of her juices to drip out.

They were absolutely magnificent.

Every time they moved their muscles rippled beneath their skin, and she wondered if she was drooling. She realized that she probably looked ridiculous turning her head back and forth between them as if she were watching a tennis match.

Tori's gaze snagged onto Bryant's cock and she drew in a ragged breath when she saw how big he was. She then turned to Jeremiah and saw he was just as big, if not a little longer. She licked her lips nervously and then looked up into Luther's eyes when he released her breast with a pop.

"Don't be scared, baby. We won't hurt you." Luther pushed to a sitting position and then he pulled his shirt up over his head and flung it aside. She followed the movement of his hand when he reached his belt buckle and released it, and then he popped the button on his jeans.

When he got off the bed she moaned with need as she saw his pectorals flex and his huge biceps bulge with each motion, and then he was pushing his jeans down. He was thicker and longer than either of his brothers and she was a bit worried.

Luther kicked his shoes and jeans off and then he got back onto the bed, his hands landing on her knees. "Do you trust us, Tori?"

Chapter Seven

She looked from brother to brother before locking gazes with Luther again. Even though she was a little intimidated and nervous about what was about to happen she realized that she did trust them, more than she'd ever thought she'd trust anyone besides Felicity.

"Yes."

Tori was shaking with desire and wanted to beg them to touch her now, but before she could voice her needs Bryant leaned over and started kissing her. She whimpered and clutched at his shoulders and then she moaned when Luther stroked his hands up the inside of her thighs, gently pushing her legs apart, and she was full of anticipation as his hands got closer to her pussy.

When a hot, wet mouth latched on to a nipple and fingers pinched the other one she cried out but the sound was muffled by Bryant's mouth. And then she cried out again when Luther stroked his finger through her hot, swollen, wet folds. Her pussy clenched and her clit throbbed. She'd never felt like this before, aching with a need so great that she felt out of control, totally mindless.

Bryant broke the kiss and then nipped and nibbled his way to her neck where he lightly sucked on her skin. She hadn't realized that her neck was an erogenous zone until that moment, but the sensation of having his mouth suckle on her skin made her a little wild. She was breathing heavily and realized the groans and moans she could hear were coming from her.

Her back arched, pushing her hips up when Luther caressed a finger around her clit, causing the ache inside to intensify. But no matter how she moved to get his touch where she wanted it, he avoided it.

"What do you want, baby?" Luther kissed the inside of her thigh and she looked down her body to meet his heat-filled, glittering gaze.

"What?" she asked on an exhalation.

Jeremiah released the nipple he'd been sucking on and shifted until his head was next to and level with hers. "Luther wants you to tell him what you want him to do to you, Tori."

She shivered as his warm breath wafted over her ear and goose bumps raced over her whole body.

"Touch me," she said in a whisper but knew they heard her when they all smiled.

"Where do you want me to touch you, baby?"

Tori's cheeks heated and she blew out a frustrated breath, because she knew damn well they knew where she wanted to be touched. Her muscles tensed for a moment as she wondered if they were playing some sort of game, but then she realized they wouldn't do that. Luther, Jeremiah, and Bryant had been straight with her from the start, but she couldn't work out why they wanted her to tell them what she wanted.

Luther must have seen the confusion on her face because he sat up between her legs and then cupped her face. "We would never do anything to hurt or make you feel ashamed, baby. We like to hear our woman talking a little dirty. It gets us excited. Okay?"

The tension in her muscles dissipated and she nodded her head. Luther leaned over and kissed her deeply. When he weaned his mouth from hers she was once again shaking with her hunger.

Luther slid back down between her legs until he was lying on his belly and his head was directly over her mound. Her back bowed, pushing her pussy higher toward his mouth when she felt his hot breath on her skin, but he just grinned at her and turned his head so that her cunt didn't come into contact with his mouth.

"Where do you want to be touched, Tori?"

Tori licked her dry lips and took a deep shuddering breath. "My pussy. I want you to touch my clit, my pussy, my breasts, and everywhere in between."

"Fuck yes," Jeremiah said and then he was kissing her.

"Mmm," Luther groaned. "You smell so sweet. I have to have a taste of this pretty little cunt."

That was the only warning she got. She cried out when Luther's tongue ran the length of her pussy from her hole up to her clit, the sound muffled by Jeremiah's mouth.

"Fucking delicious." Luther growled against her folds, which sent vibrations down deep to her womb and even to her ass.

Bryant licked over one of her nipples and then he scraped his teeth across the tip, which made her pussy clench and release more of her juices. And then she groaned when Luther's tongue lapped over her clit.

His hot, moist tongue felt so good she thought she just might die from too much pleasure. He licked and sucked at her until her limbs were shaking and her toes curled. She'd never felt anything like the rapture being bestowed on her and didn't think she would with any other man.

But then she was even more astounded because Luther pushed the tip of a finger into her pussy and the exquisite sensations got even better. Jeremiah lifted his mouth from hers and then he, too, was suckling at her nipple. He didn't lick and lap at her peak like Bryant had at first. He sucked her hard peak into his mouth and suckled on her strongly. That little bite of pain had her writhing beneath them and crying out for more.

Luther's finger pushed into her all the way and after pausing a moment he slid it back out. She wanted to beg him to put it back in and just as she opened her mouth to do just that he came back with two fingers. The pressure was intense as her delicate, wet tissue spread. She'd seen how thick and long his fingers were and she bowed her hips from the bed to get more of those pleasure-giving digits inside her. He lifted his mouth from her pussy and placed the palm of his hand on her lower abdomen and applied firm yet gentle pressure to hold her down.

"Easy, baby. We'll give you what you need." Luther's voice was more gravelly than usual and it was then that she realized he was as turned on as she was. His control astounded her and she knew he and his brothers would never do anything to deliberately hurt her. In fact they all seemed hell-bent on making sure she felt only pleasure.

Tori hadn't even realized that she was still a little wary until that moment and she wanted to tell Luther, Jeremiah, and Bryant that she really did trust them. But the words wouldn't come because she was so full of emotion she was scared she would start crying, so she nodded instead and gave herself over into their care.

Luther's green eyes met hers and he smiled at her as if he knew what she'd just been thinking and how she'd given them all the control.

"That's it, baby. Just relax and feel." He lowered his head back to her cunt, and as he licked over her engorged pearl he pushed his fingers into her deeper. He didn't shove them in all the way. No, he took care of her and slowly pumped them in and out until they were in as far as they would go. He paused and then as he sucked her clit in between his lips and lapped over it with his tongue, he began to stroke those wonderfully thick fingers in and out of her pussy. With each press forward he got faster and faster and the pads of his digits stroked over a spot inside her that nearly sent her to the roof.

"Such a sexy woman," Jeremiah whispered and then he sucked her nipple back into his mouth.

Bryant reached up and held her breast in his large hand and bit down on her nipple. That small zing of pain made her insides tighten and it felt like heated wine was coursing through her veins. She cried out as her pussy fluttered and cream dripped from her hole. Never in her life had Tori experienced...

Thoughts flew right out of her head. That heated wine now felt like it was burning her from the inside. She gasped for breath and then she screamed. Her womb shivered, her cunt trembled and tightened, and then she was flying toward the stars.

Her internal muscles clamped around Luther's fingers as he thrust them in and out of her body. Her whole body quaked and quivered as she went hurtling up into the stratosphere. The climax seemed to last forever, but it was over way to soon.

When Tori came back to herself it was to find three sets of eyes staring at her hungrily and they were caressing their hands over her body. She panted and gulped at the intense look in their eyes and wondered if they would want to fuck her now.

God, I hope so. Please, please want me the way I want you.

* * * *

Luther was so damn horny he was shaking. He'd never felt this way about a woman before and knew he never would again. Seeing Tori in the throes of climax was the highlight of his life and the only thing that would be better was being able to make love with her.

He didn't think she was a virgin, but from the shocked and awed look he'd seen cross her face just before she came, she was sexually inexperienced. Possessiveness roared through him and it was hell to keep from sheathing his cock in a condom and thrusting into her until his balls rested against her ass. He wanted to reassure her how sexy she was when she came but didn't think his voice would work if he tried to talk. Tori looked a little vulnerable and when he met her gaze and saw tears in her eyes he felt like a real bastard.

Did I hurt her? Was I too rough with her?

He took a deep breath and glanced at his brothers. They must have seen the shimmer of tears in her eyes too, because they were both frowning and looked really worried.

"Tori, are you okay?"

Tori nodded and gave a delicate sniff.

Luther sat up between her legs and caressed a hand over her belly. The muscles beneath her skin jumped and he wondered if it was because she liked his touch or if she was having second thoughts.

"Did I hurt you, baby?"

"No," Tori whispered and looked away as red infused her cheeks.

Jeremiah cupped her face and turned her head toward him. "Why are you crying?"

"I've never…"

Bryant shifted at her side and the frown left his face. Luther realized then what Tori was trying to say and the tension eased from his muscles.

"No one's ever made you come before?" Bryant asked.

Tori eyelids lowered as if she was trying to hide from them, but she nodded her head and confirmed what he'd thought she had been trying to say.

"Did you like it?" Luther bit his lip to stop the smile from forming on his mouth.

Tori's mouth opened and then closed and then she gave him the most beautiful smile he'd ever seen. "Hell yes."

Her answer was so emphatic he couldn't hold his smile back anymore. In fact he ended up laughing, as did Jeremiah and Bryant.

"Can we do that again?"

"We can do that whenever you want, darlin'." Bryant brushed a strand of hair off her face.

"We want to make love with you, Tori," Luther said but held up his hand when she opened her mouth to reply. He knew he'd already told her that if she accepted being with them that there would be no turning back, but he wanted to make sure she understood unequivocally what they wanted with her. "If you agree to this going forward you need to know that you'll be ours from then on. Don't say yes unless you're absolutely sure that's what you want."

Tori nibbled on her lip, still looking very vulnerable and uncertain. Luther would have loved to know what was going through her head right then, but women's minds often worked in mysterious ways. He didn't think he'd ever be confident enough to know what Tori was thinking. She was a gorgeous, sexy woman, but she was also an enigma, at least to him. He glanced at Jeremiah and he looked just as uncertain as Tori, but when he looked at Bryant his younger brother was smiling.

"Darlin', we want you more than our next breath, but if you're unsure we should stop now."

Luther wanted to hit his brother for saying that, but he knew Bryant was right. If Tori had any misgivings about being with them they needed to clear them up before taking the next step.

"I want you all," Tori said and then took a deep breath.

"But?" Jeremiah asked.

"I don't know if I'm the right woman for you. What if I can't give you what you need?"

Luther cursed under his breath. Tori had been hurt before and from what she'd just said not only by her mother and stepfather. Some egotistical motherfucker had hurt her and made her feel less confident as a stunning, healthy, sexual woman. He wanted her to tell him the asshole's name so he could go and punch the shit out of him, but he held his anger in check so he didn't scare her.

"Baby, if you don't give us what we need then it's our own fault."

Tori frowned at him in confusion.

"It's our job to make sure that you're satisfied, Tori. If you are gratified then so are we."

"But..."

Jeremiah placed a finger over her lips. "No buts, honey."

"Do you want to be with us, Tori? Do you want us to make love with you?"

Again she frowned, but this time Luther knew it was over his word choice. He wasn't about to tell her that he was well on the way to falling in love with her or that he and his brothers having sex with her wasn't just sex or fucking. To them it would be making love, but Luther was certain that she wasn't ready to hear any of that yet.

Hopefully he and his brothers would be able to bolster her confidence once they'd all made love with her and she would lose the vulnerability regarding her own femininity.

Luther didn't realize that he was clenching his fist until his knuckles started aching. He saw Jeremiah exhale and then inhale deeply as if he'd been holding his breath, and Bryant had a frown on his face where usually he was smiling.

He and his brothers knew that their future depended on the answer Tori gave, but if she said no he wasn't going to walk away with his tail between his legs. She was the epitome of everything they wanted in a woman. Tori Springer was beautiful, sexy, and deep down he had a feeling that when she gave her heart it would be for the rest of her life.

He'd seen the yearning in her eyes when she watched Flick and her husbands. When Tom, Billy, and Luke touched her in passing or kissed Felicity on the cheek, the need that appeared in her eyes, the need to be loved, was there for anyone to see.

She wasn't like any of the women he and his brothers had dated. Thank God. She didn't use her sexuality to get what she wanted. She didn't look at any other man the way she looked at them. Not even the handsome Trick Wendall and his brothers drew an appreciative gaze from Tori. The women they'd known would have been hanging all over the Wendall brothers trying to get their attention. But Tori wasn't like that.

She was sweet and caring and he wanted to have those traits of hers directed at them. Once he, Jeremiah, and Bryant had her where they wanted her there was no way in hell he was going to ever let her go.

She was theirs, and Luther was going to make damn sure she was by their sides until they breathed their last breaths.

Chapter Eight

Jeremiah was scared she was going to say no. He could see the cogs of her mind turning, but he couldn't work out what she was thinking. Even though her face and eyes showed a myriad of emotions he couldn't tell if she was going to refuse or accept them.

Her face had gone pink a moment ago in what looked like embarrassment and then had paled and she'd frowned. The last few minutes had been the longest of his life and he couldn't deal with the silence a moment longer. Usually Luther would have pushed for an answer by now. His older brother could be a real impatient bastard, just like he could. Even Bryant looked upset, his usual smile a frown.

"Talk to us, honey? What has you hesitating?"

"I–I'm not very good with relationships. I…I don't want to come between you all."

"That would never happen, darlin'." Bryant gave her a gentle smile and took her hand in his and then laced their fingers together.

"But…" Tori hesitated.

Jeremiah had had enough of the pussyfooting around. He would probably catch hell from Bryant and maybe Luther for pushing later, but he needed to know her uncertainties, her fears, so he could allay them for her.

"How many boyfriends have you had, Tori?"

"Jeremiah," Luther snapped and Jeremiah glared at his brother when Tori looked intimidated from Luther's tone. "What the hell did you ask that for?"

"Fuck you, Luther. I wasn't trying to embarrass her or make her feel bad," Jeremiah said with a snarl. "I wanted…"

"See, I knew this couldn't work."

Tori sat up and was about to scramble around Jeremiah and off the bed, but he couldn't let her escape. At least not yet. He snagged her around the waist as he shifted on the bed so he was sitting on the edge and then plopped her down on his lap. He had to bite back the groan that was forming in his chest when her warm, soft ass cheeks and hip brushed against his hard cock.

"What are you doing?" Tori pushed against the arm he had around her waist. "Let me go."

"Not yet." Jeremiah breathed in her strawberry scent and kissed the top of her head. She smelled so good he started drooling, but now was not the time for lascivious thoughts so he pushed them aside. It was imperative that he and his brothers get to the heart of her trepidation and deal with those issues before they could move forward.

"Answer my question, Tori."

Tori huffed out an agitated breath and glared daggers at him, but she did finally answer the question, even if it was a little pithily. "Two."

"Okay." Jeremiah was getting a clearer picture and he didn't like what he was seeing, but he needed to know the rest. "How many times have you had sex?"

The anger in her eyes went to discomfit and complete fury. Instead of pushing against his arm this time she pinched it and he drew back in surprise. She jumped from his lap and started gathering her clothes. Luther and Bryant were glaring at him and even though he hated making her mad and uncomfortable Jeremiah knew that until all the skeletons were out of her closet she wasn't going to relax totally with them.

Tori pulled on her clothes with jerky movements and Jeremiah figured she would be more at ease if they were all dressed, too, so he started getting dressed. Luther and Bryant put their clothes back on as well.

Jeremiah had finished before Tori, and while she'd been concentrating on doing her jeans up and slipping her feet into her shoes, he'd walked over to the bedroom door and was now leaning against his with his arms crossed over his chest. When she took a step toward the door and then noticed where he was she scowled at him and placed her hands on her hips in an offensive move.

"Please get out of the way," Tori stated more than asked.

He shook his head. "You're not leaving until we've talked, Tori. I can stand here all night if I have to."

She glared at him and he held her stare. With a sigh she finally looked down toward the floor.

"I've had sex twice," she snapped and met his eyes again. Her tone had been really belligerent and she thrust her chin into the air as if she expected him to belittle her inexperience.

"With the same man or two different men?" Jeremiah shoved from the door and uncrossed his arms before taking a step toward her. Even though Luther and Bryant were still looking at him angrily they kept quiet. Maybe they were finally working out what he was trying to do.

"The same man."

"You didn't have sex with your first boyfriend?"

"No."

"Why not?"

"I'm not a slut, Jeremiah. I don't go around spreading my legs for anything with a cock."

He held in his smirk when her face went bright red at what she'd said, but he didn't comment on her use of words.

"We know very well you're not a slut, honey. We wouldn't want to be with you if we thought you were."

She let out what sounded like a sigh of relief and her next words confirmed it. "Thank God for small mercies."

"Your one and only lover didn't give you an orgasm, did he, Tori?"

Her hands moved from her hips and she wiped them down the front of her thighs as if she was nervous, but she shook her head.

"Did he say it was your fault you couldn't come?" Jeremiah asked her in a quiet voice.

Tori shook her head, but then she changed it to a nod and her gaze once more went to the floor. Her cheeks went a deep red hue this time. Jeremiah's heart ached for her. He wondered how long she'd had the misconception that there was something wrong with her. God, he hated assholes like her ex. Why did some men have to hurt and belittle women to cover up their own insecurities, inadequacies?

"Whatever he said to you, he was wrong." Jeremiah took the last few steps until he was standing in front of her and then he slowly reached out and nudged her chin up. "There is nothing wrong or lacking in you, Tori. He was the inadequate one."

Luther and Bryant moved closer to her, too. Luther placed his hands on her shoulders and pulled her back against his front. Bryant took her hand in his, raised it to his mouth, and kissed the back of it.

"What did that fucker tell you, baby?" Luther asked.

"He told me I wasn't w–woman enough." Tori's voice hitched and then she swallowed audibly.

"What else did he say, darlin'?" Bryant caressed his free hand down her arm.

"He said it was my fault he had to go looking for sex with another woman when we were supposed to be going out. If I hadn't been cold he would never have cheated on me."

"Fucking asshole," Jeremiah snapped and then stroked a finger down her cheek when she flinched. "I'm sorry, honey. I didn't mean to scare you."

"You didn't. Not really." Tori finally met his eyes again. "You just surprised me, is all."

"Let's get something straight," Jeremiah began. "You are not lacking in any way, sexually or otherwise. You are a very intelligent, gorgeous, sexy woman and we want to be in a relationship with you."

Tori opened her mouth, but Jeremiah rubbed his thumb over her bottom lip to stop her. Her breath puffed out onto his skin and she licked her lips and that sweet pink little tongue connected with his thumb. He wanted to strip her down again, toss her on the bed, and love her until they were both screaming, but Tori wasn't ready for that yet. She hadn't really been ready for them loving her before, but now that they were at the crux of her insecurities hopefully he and his brothers could help make her ready.

"We want to see where this attraction between us will lead, honey. Luther, Bryant, and I want to have it all. We want to settle down in our own home and hopefully have a few kids and we think you could be the woman we want to settle down with."

"You do?"

Jeremiah was pleased when his brothers got on board with him. Tori needed to know that they wanted her in their lives forever. It was no wonder she was so uncertain after her upbringing and the two assholes she'd gone out with. Now that she knew the score hopefully she would want what they wanted, too.

"I—"

"Don't say anything just now, baby. We know you're going to be busy with your new shop and so are we if we can find a place we want to buy." Luther tugged on her ponytail and Tori tilted her head back to look at him. "Just know that we will always be here for you. Okay?"

Tori's breath hitched and her chin wobbled, but she managed to answer even if her voice trembled a little. Jeremiah was worried for a moment. That was until he realized she was overcome with emotion.

"Thank you. No one's ever really been there for me before, besides Felicity, and we didn't really have a chance to socialize much since we both had a similar upbringing."

"Do you have your cell phone, darlin'?" Bryant asked.

Luther loosened his hold around Tori's waist when she dug into her pocket and pulled her phone out, before handing it to Bryant.

"I'm going to put our cell numbers in your phone on speed dial. If you need us or just want to chat, don't even think of hesitating to call us." Bryant glanced up from her cell and met her gaze. "Do you understand?"

"Yes."

"We don't care what time it is," Jeremiah said. "Day or night no matter what the hour. Okay?"

"Yes."

"Good," Luther said. "Now why don't we walk you back to the house, so you can get some rest?"

"I don't need you to come with me. I'm a big girl." Tori smiled.

"We know, honey, but we like to see our dates safely to the door." He reached out, grabbed her hand, and led her out. Jeremiah just hoped it wouldn't be too long before they saw or heard from Tori again.

The only way she could get to know them was by spending more time with them. But it was going to be difficult with them all starting the next step on the path of new careers. Jeremiah was just glad she was still living in the guest room of the ranch house. If she wasn't he had a feeling they would hardly see her at all.

* * * *

The next four weeks flew by for Tori, but they also seemed to drag. She and Trick were so busy with refurbishing the shop and painting. She was just glad that Trick's brothers, Trent and Tristan, were in the construction business because Trick had commandeered them to help outfit the store and they got their services at a cheaper rate. Once they had the shelves, display cabinets, and clothing racks set up they'd set out stock and had hardly had a moment to themselves.

Tori looked out the window as she painted the timber window frame. When she saw movement across the road she squinted against the sun's glare and saw a man leaning against the tree watching her. A chill ran up and down her spine and she looked around for Trick, but when she couldn't see him she turned back to the window. The guy was no longer looking at her but down the street. At first she'd been a little concerned but she pushed her worry aside when she realized he was probably just curious about what she and Trick were doing and what sort of shop they were going to open. When he walked away, she chuckled under her breath at her own paranoia and was glad she hadn't called Trick over, and made a fool of herself.

She finished painting and moved on to the next job on her list.

Tori had read so many instruction manuals her head was spinning. If she had to read another instruction leaflet about how to put a baby's cot together, she may just end up running through the street screaming. It was really hard to work things out when the instructions were written grammatically incorrect, but she'd persevered and triumphed in the end.

The only time she got to spend with Luther, Jeremiah, and Bryant was at dinner time, but she was so tired by the end of each day she wasn't very good company.

But she'd been happy for them when they'd found a place to buy, and the three Katz brothers were also busy fixing up the ranch house and getting the paddocks ready so they could bring in some cattle.

Tori was glad that Felicity's morning, afternoon, and evening sickness with her pregnancy seemed to have settled down. She hadn't had the chance to do any cooking or cleaning for her. Flick's husbands had taken over those chores until their wife was feeling better.

The grand opening for Mom's and Bub's was tomorrow and even though she should have been zonked out by now, Tori was too excited to sleep. She turned her pillow over again and rolled to her side, but no matter how hard she tried to relax she couldn't. After flinging the covers aside she pulled her track pants on beneath her large T-shirt and headed to the kitchen. She got a glass of water and took it out onto the verandah and breathed in the fresh, crisp night air. Tori just hoped that now everything was set up that she wouldn't have to spend nearly every waking moment working at the store. With any luck now she could work more regular hours and get to spend more time with Luther, Jeremiah, and Bryant.

When she glanced toward the far bunkhouse she saw that there was a light on inside. She wanted to go over there and visit but decided it was too late. It was already close to midnight and she was meeting Trick at the shop tomorrow morning at seven.

Tori turned her head toward the end of the verandah when she heard a noise and her heart pounded hard in her chest when she saw the shadow of a large man walking toward her. Her breath was choppy and she placed her hand on her chest, trying to calm her racing heart.

"Tori, what are you doing out here?" Luther asked as he drew closer to the steps and then came up them. He must have seen her hand and realized he'd frightened her. "I didn't mean to scare you, baby. Sorry."

"It's okay. I couldn't see who was out here and got a little nervous."

"Why aren't you in bed asleep?"

"I'm too anxious."

Luther stopped in front of her and then gestured toward the cushion beside her. "Do you mind if I sit down?"

"Sure."

"Is everything set for the opening tomorrow?" Luther asked after he was seated.

"Yes. As much as it can be."

"I'm sorry we haven't been in to help you or take a peek, but we've been busy. Now that the house is finished and the paddocks are all fenced off we should be able to keep better hours. Although we have a shipment of cattle coming in tomorrow afternoon."

"Wow, you guys must have been working flat chat?"

"We have." Luther took her free hand in his and started playing with her fingers. "We're going to come by in the morning for a bit of moral support."

"Thank you, that means a lot."

"You mean a lot to us, baby." Luther cleared his throat. "Have you thought about what you want yet, Tori?"

"Yes."

"And have you made any decisions?"

"Yes." Tori swallowed nervously. "I'd really like to have a relationship with you."

"You would?" Luther sounded as if her answer was unexpected and he was relieved.

"Yes."

Luther's hands landed at her waist and she gave a squeak of surprise when he lifted her onto his lap. His lips brushed against hers and then he whispered against her mouth. "Thank you, baby. I promise you won't regret your decision."

And then he was kissing her. He didn't start off slow, but devoured her from the first meeting of lips. His tongue plunged into her mouth, twirling with hers until they were both moaning and panting. Luther lifted his head and stared deeply into her eyes. "God, I've missed you. Will you let me make you feel good? Maybe you'll be able to sleep afterward."

"Yes. Please," Tori replied and then leaned forward so she could kiss him. Their tongues mated and he ran his hand up and down her body. When he cupped her breast and thrummed her hard nipple she arched into his touch. But it wasn't enough. She needed to feel his warm skin and hard muscles under her hands, and his large hands on her bare skin.

Tori slipped her hand beneath the hem of his shirt and caressed him all over. She loved the feeling of his heat and body beneath her hand and she stroked up until she reached the pinhead-sized nipple and pinched it between her finger and thumb.

Luther broke the kiss and nuzzled her neck with his nose. "Fuck, baby. You've got me so hard."

"I'll say." Tori giggled as she wiggled on his lap.

"You little minx. I'll get you back for that."

"Promises, promises," Tori said and was surprised by her own playfulness. She'd never been this way before but she liked it. Hopefully now that she'd decided she wanted to be with them she would be more relaxed. She liked this side of herself and it seemed that Luther did, too.

He copied her moves and smoothed his hand up over her stomach and then cupped her braless breast. She moaned and arched into his palm, silently begging for more. He flicked her nipple with his thumb and her pussy clenched in reaction, leaking cream out onto her panties. And then his hand moved back down and pushed beneath the elastic of her sweatpants and panties.

His mouth slanted over hers just as his fingers slid through her wet folds and muffled the groan that erupted from deep in her chest. When he pushed a finger up inside her cunt she bowed up into his touch and blindly felt at his waistband for his belt buckle. She fumbled with it a few times and was pleased when Luther helped her out by opening the clasp and then she took over again. She pulled the button on his jeans open and carefully lowered the zipper over his massively erect cock.

Tori pushed her hand into his shorts and wrapped it around his erection, pumping it a few times. Her hand slipped from his cock when he lifted her off of his lap and then he pushed his jeans and boxers down to the top of his thighs, before her ass landed on the cushion beside him.

"I need you so bad, baby. I've never felt like this before. I feel almost…desperate to be inside you."

Tori felt the same way and craved to know what his cock would feel like as he slid in and out of her wet pussy.

"Do you have any protection?"

"Yes."

"Get it," Tori commanded. There was no way she could go to sleep when she ached so badly for his touch.

"Are you sure, baby? You don't have to do this."

"I want to. I need you, Luther."

Luther stood up, dug into his pocket for the condom, and then he pushed his jeans and underwear down to his ankles. He ripped open the foil pack and then rolled the latex down over his penis. When he was done he reached for her again and pushed the sweatpants and panties she was wearing over her hips, down her legs, and she kicked them aside.

He picked her up and sat back down on the small outdoor sofa. She ended up with her knees in the cushion on either side of his body, facing him as she straddled his hips. Luther shifted one of his hands back between her legs and caressed her pussy from her clit down to her hole and back up to her clit again. He rubbed the tip of his finger over the enlarged sensitive nub a few times.

"So wet for me, baby. Do you want my cock inside your pussy?"

"Yes," Tori said on a low moan. "Hurry."

And then she took a deep breath and held it when she felt the tip of his condom-covered cock at her entrance. Both of his hands were now back on her hips and he gently pulled her down. She groaned with frustration when his hard dick slipped away from her cunt, but then his hand brushed against her as he reached between her legs and held it upright.

"Take me inside you, Tori," Luther panted.

Tori slowly lowered herself down and moaned when he began to penetrate her pussy. He was so big her walls stretched to permit him and she felt a slight burning sensation.

"Nice and easy, baby. Just go slow." His deep, gravelly voice washed over her, causing her whole body to shiver as goose bumps formed over her skin.

"Fuck. So hot, wet, and tight."

"Oh God, Luther. You feel so good." Tori moved up and down, gaining inch after inch of his hard cock inside her cunt. By the time she had him all the way inside her she was filled to capacity and quaking with need.

"Are you ready, babe? Are you ready for me?" Luther rasped.

"Yes, I need you, Luther. Help me, I don't know what to do."

His hold on his hips became firmer, but not enough to hurt her or leave any marks, and then he slowly lifted her up from his body until just the tip of his cock was still inside her. Tori was so hungry for him she didn't want slow. When he started pulling her back down, she let gravity take over and slammed down onto him.

"Damn, Tori. Don't do that. I don't want to hurt you," Luther panted.

"You won't." She gasped. "I need you deep inside me. I want fast and hard, Luther."

Luther made a low, growly noise in his throat and then he wrapped his arms around her, rose to his feet, and carried her away from the sofa. He spun around and pressed her back against the side of the house.

"Tell me if I hurt you," were the last words he spoke before he began pumping his hips.

Tori bit her lip and tried to keep the moans and groans from escaping her mouth as Luther began to fuck her. His cock slid in and out of her pussy over and over again. Each time his pelvis connected with hers he ground against her clit. The sensations of having his cock shuttling in and out of her cunt were unbelievably exquisite. Their lower bodies slapped together with each rock of their hips and the pressure building inside her was overwhelming.

She'd never felt anything like this before and hoped she would again very, very soon.

His cock caressed her snug walls so exquisitely and the friction of each stroke sent her higher and higher and higher. Her muscles fluttered around his hard penis and cream continually dripped from her cunt.

Luther's hands kneaded and spread her ass cheeks, causing a slight sting in her back hole, but that only made the pleasure greater. And then he was pumping into her faster and harder, grunting each time their bodies slammed together.

Tension seeped into every muscle until her body was so taut she thought she may just break. And then she did.

Luther slanted his mouth over hers, his tongue pushing in to glide along hers as he pounded into her. She shattered. Her cunt clamped and released, quaked and quavered on his cock as rapture assailed her whole body. She shivered and shook and cried out as cum gushed from her pussy.

He thrust into her twice more and then froze, and he groaned as his cock heated even more, expanded slightly inside her as he spumed cum into the end of the condom. Tori slumped against the side of the house in languid satiation, glad that he had the strength to hold her up. Even though her arms were wrapped around his neck and her legs around his waist, she had no strength left. She felt as limp as a wet noodle.

Luther lifted his mouth from hers and rested his forehead against hers as they both panted for breath.

"You're amazing, Tori." Luther kissed her lightly on the lips. "Thank you, baby."

Tori lowered her legs and was glad he held her steady as she got her equilibrium back, because she wobbled a bit. She winced at the tenderness between her thighs and unhooked her arms from around his neck. It was only then she realized that they were out in the open where anyone could have seen them. The only consolation was that she still had her large sleeping T-shirt on and it had fallen to mid-thigh as she lowered her legs. She was completely covered. She'd never done anything like that before and was a little embarrassed at how carried away she'd been. She just hoped that none of the ranch hands had heard or seen them. Tori scanned the yard and was relieved when she didn't see anyone and all the lights in the other bunkhouse were off.

Thank God, she'd been worrying over nothing. At least that's what she hoped.

Luther stepped back, picked up his clothes, and put them back on before turning toward her again.

"We're moving to our own place on Sunday." He paused to take a breath. "Would you come with us?"

"You're moving?" Tori gulped, hoping he couldn't hear the hurt in her voice.

He cupped her face between his hands. "We want you to move in with us, baby."

"I–I don't know…"

"Tori, you agreed to be in a relationship with us. We can get to know each other better if you move in."

"What if it doesn't work out?" Tori blurted out her innermost fear.

"It will." Luther kissed her forehead. "We've hardly seen each other over the last month. We've all been so busy, but now that the house renovations are done, we want more than that with you, baby. We want you with us all the time."

Now that she had decided to be with them and had sex with Luther, she wanted so much more. And he was right. They were all so busy with their new careers the only way to see each other was if she moved in with them. She didn't want to have a few stolen moments with Luther, Jeremiah, and Bryant on the weekend.

Tori wanted everything with them because she had gone and done the one thing she vowed she'd never do.

She'd fallen in love with the Katz brothers.

Chapter Nine

Bryant was glad that Tori was moving in with them. He'd been a little envious that Luther had made love to their woman, but he knew his and Jeremiah's time was coming. He just hoped it would be soon. They'd worked their asses off getting the house livable and all the fencing and barns up to par.

He, Luther, and Jeremiah had gone to the grand opening of Mom's and Bub's and had been astounded with what they saw. The whole shop was dedicated to pregnant women, women with kids and babies. There were furniture displays, linens and blankets for the cots and cribs, and also maternity and baby clothes. He'd never seen so much of that stuff in one place before. He guessed there were similar stores in other towns and cities, but he'd never taken much notice.

Hopefully one day he and his brothers along with Tori would be able to go shopping for baby things, too. Bryant had dropped into the shop yesterday since he'd needed to go to town for some supplies and he'd taken lunch for Tori. She'd seemed a little distracted and kept looking out the window and glancing around as if she were nervous. At first he'd thought she was worried about what customers would think seeing him in the shop talking to her, but he knew when she kissed him that he was wrong. But there was something going on with her and he wanted to know what. For this relationship to work between the four of them they had to communicate about everything. He'd wanted to ask what was distressing her but more customers had entered the shop and he didn't think it was appropriate to have that conversation when others could overhear.

He was currently standing on the verandah at the front of the house waiting for Luther and Tori to arrive while sipping on a mug of coffee. Luther had gone over to the Double E Ranch to help her move her things and Jeremiah was putting the finishing touches to Tori's room and bathroom.

The ranch house had six bedrooms. Four rooms were at one end of the house and two at the other. He and his brothers had put in a new en-suite bathroom off the master bedroom. Their intention was to all sleep in the one room, so they'd made sure there was enough closet space for all of them as well as a custom-made bed to fit them all, too. He just hoped that Tori liked the color scheme, but if not it wouldn't take the three of them long to repaint it with colors she liked. Bryant anticipated that he would get to spend some time with their woman in the adjacent bathroom. The shower was big enough for six people with multiple showerheads set at different heights and angles and the spa bath was also more than big enough for all of them.

He was as anxious as a kid on his first day at school. Bryant couldn't wait to wrap her up in his arms and hold her tight. When he heard a car in the distance he straightened up from his slouched leaning position on the rail and called out to Jeremiah.

"They're here."

"Shit," Jeremiah yelled and Bryant could hear his brother's feet on the polished timber floors as he headed to the porch. The screen door slammed open and then Jeremiah walked out with a cup of coffee in his hand and portrayed a relaxed pose that he was far from feeling. His knuckles were white as he gripped the handle of the cup.

"Do you think she'll like her bedroom? Do you think she'll let us sleep in there with her?"

"How should I know?" Bryant replied and smiled. Jeremiah and Luther had been anxious over everything the last few days, and even though he felt the same, it was amusing to see his arrogant older brothers unsure of themselves for a change.

Luther pulled his truck up close to the house and Tori did the same with her small SUV. He and Jeremiah placed their mugs on the top of the rail and hurried down to Tori's car. Bryant beat his older brother by a mere pace and then he opened Tori's door for her.

"Hey, darlin', how are you?" Bryant helped her out of the car and pulled her into his arms. He was pleased when she wrapped her arms around his waist and hugged him tight.

Her forehead was pressed into his chest and her voice was muffled when she spoke, but he heard her. "I've missed you."

Bryant sighed with relief. He wasn't sure how she was going to react to them all since she'd had sex with Luther. He'd thought she may be a little shy but was glad that didn't seem to be the case. "I've missed you, too. You don't know how happy you've made me by coming to live with us." He drew back and stared at her beautiful face and vowed to do everything he could to make her happy. "Why don't you go inside and get settled? We'll bring your stuff in."

"I can help," Tori said and turned to do just that, and before he could stop her Jeremiah shoved him out of the way and lifted her off her feet and cradled her in his arms.

"Don't I get a hello, too?" Jeremiah's voice was even, but Bryant could see the hurt in his eyes.

"Jer, I didn't even know you were there." Tori wrapped her arms around Jer's neck and then kissed him on the cheek before pointing at Bryant. "This big lug hid you from my view."

Bryant smiled and gave her a wink before starting to unload the cases from her car. Jeremiah needed some time with Tori, too.

"I'm happy to see you, honey. You look tired."

Tori nodded. "I've been real busy."

Jeremiah swung her up into his arms and spun in a circle. Tori shrieked then laughed, clutching at him around the neck. He laughed and then stopped spinning, and then he lowered her to her feet making sure her body slid down his. He looked down into her eyes and smiled, because she was still smiling and he loved seeing her that way. But when he noticed the way her eyes changed from happiness to desire he couldn't resist. Slowly he lowered his head, so she would have time to move away if she wanted, and when she didn't he brushed his lips back and forth over hers. She sighed and melted into him and then they were kissing wildly, passionately, rapaciously.

Bryant couldn't get over the way Jeremiah had started playing with her. His brother had never done that before, but now that they were kissing he wanted in on the action, too. As he took a step toward her Luther came back out of the house after carrying her suitcases inside.

"Hey, we need to get Tori's stuff inside."

When Bryant looked at Luther he could see the lust and yearning in his eyes. His big brother wanted to kiss, cuddle, and love Tori, too. But outside where anyone could see them wasn't the place. They didn't have any ranch hands yet, but there were always trucks going past their place as they went into Slick Rock for supplies. The last thing they needed was to make Tori self-conscious and uncomfortable.

Jeremiah slowed the kiss down until he was sipping at Tori's lips and then lowered her back to her feet. She took a couple of deep breaths to get her breathing back under control and then turned back to her car.

"Tori, go inside with Bryant. Jer and I will finish unloading your stuff," Luther commanded.

Tori frowned at him. "I can—"

"Do as you're told." Luther pointed toward the door and then turned away again.

Bryant could tell that she was a little hurt by Luther's attitude, but he would explain it to her once he took her inside. He clasped her hand and tugged lightly, and after huffing out a frustrated breath she followed him reluctantly. Tori took in the living room and then the kitchen. After guiding her to a stool at the counter he started making coffee.

"Luther isn't angry with you, darlin'."

"He sure sounded angry."

"He's horny, Tori. We all are. We want you so much."

"There was no need for him to talk to me that way."

Bryant sighed. "No, you're right, there wasn't. You have us all tied up in knots, darlin'."

"So, it's my fault?" Tori crossed her arms beneath her breasts, which drew his eyes to her cleavage. When she noticed where he was looking she dropped her arms and quirked an eyebrow at him. He'd never seen such a sexy look on her face before and his softening cock twitched and then filled quickly with blood. He wanted to pick her up, carry her to the master bedroom, strip her down, and fuck her until neither of them could walk, but he wasn't sure she was ready for all of them yet. And he knew if he started something his brothers would be in that bedroom with him loving on her.

"No." Bryant placed the mug of coffee on the counter in front of her and then walked around the bench to sit beside her. He needed to change the subject so he could get his hunger under control. The last thing he wanted to do was scare her with the intensity of his—*their* desire.

"How's the new shop going?"

"Wonderful." She smiled. "We've been so busy that even Trick's had to come in and help out. He wanted to stay a silent partner, but until we hire some employees he's been working alongside me, every day."

"I'm happy for you, darlin'." Bryant took a swig of his coffee but glanced her way when she shifted in her seat. He inhaled deeply and knew the reason for her restlessness was because she was aroused. He could smell her sweet, musky scent.

He leaned over, licked and then nipped her earlobe. "Do you want me, Tori?"

Her cheeks flamed with color and she glanced at him and then looked down at the counter before nodding.

"Good." Bryant couldn't stay away from her any longer. He had to have her. *Now.*

He stood up, scooped her up into his arms, kicked the stool aside, and placed her ass on the counter. After pushing the mugs of coffee aside he slanted his mouth over hers. The twirl and glide of her tongue against his had him on the edge in seconds, but there was no way he was coming before her. With an alacrity he couldn't stem, he pushed her shirt up, broke the kiss, and then whipped it over her head. She shoved her hands under his shirt and ran them up over his pecs and then down over his stomach. When she reached his belt buckle he didn't stop her. She had his jeans unbuttoned and unzipped before he flicked the clasp of her bra. After he had her bra off and was working on her jeans, his knees nearly buckled when she shoved her hand into his boxers and wrapped her hand around his cock. Bryant gripped her wrist and drew her hand away. She met his gaze as she puffed out a frustrated breath.

"I want this to last, darlin'," he panted. "You've got me too wired."

Tori nodded, and as he placed an arm around her waist to lift her butt from the counter and push her jeans and panties over her hips, he latched his mouth onto one of her nipples. The little berry responded beautifully, engorging with blood and hardening to perfection. He sucked, licked, and nipped at her nipples, alternating from one to the other as he pushed her jeans down her legs. He grunted in frustration when he couldn't push them off and realized she still had her shoes on. Bryant released her nipple with a pop and then he grabbed first one ankle and then the other, removing her shoes, and then he tugged the rest of her clothes off.

"So fucking beautiful. I need to taste your honey, darlin'."

Bryant wrapped his arms around her upper thighs, lifted her legs, and pulled until her ass was on the edge of the counter and then he dove down between her legs. He licked, sucked, and laved, and relished the moaning whimpering sounds she made as she lay supine on the counter for his eager delectation. He was aware the moment Luther and Jeremiah entered the kitchen and glanced their way as they made a beeline straight for Tori. He looked at her and his breath caught in his throat at how gorgeous she looked spread out before him, totally naked with her neck arched, her eyes closed, and the pink tinge of passion flushing her skin.

Luther and Jer moved around to the other side of the counter. Luther gently lifted her head off the granite and then kissed her. Jeremiah began pinching and plucking at one hard dusky-rose nipple while suckling on the other.

Bryant pushed a finger up inside her hot, wet cunt and his balls drew up close to his body, and pre-cum leaked from his dick. He couldn't wait any longer. He needed to be inside her and was glad that he'd taken a condom from his jeans pocket and placed it on the counter before he'd started making love to her. With fumbling fingers and a shaky hand he brought the pack to his mouth and ripped it open with his teeth, and then rolled it down over his dick.

"Do you want me, darlin'? Do you want my cock inside your pretty little cunt?"

She made a humming sound that was muffled by Luther's mouth, but that was all the assent he needed. Bryant moved in closer to her, gripped the base of his cock, and rubbed it through her juices, and then he started pushing inside. He didn't surge in with one stroke because he didn't want to hurt her. He wasn't a small man and he needed to take his time with her.

His head tipped back and he moaned as her wet heat enveloped him. It felt so damn good he couldn't stop shaking. Slowly but surely he forged his way inside until his balls were flush with her ass. His muscles and tendons felt like they were standing out in stark relief now that he was all the way inside her. When she wiggled her hips he knew she was ready for him to start moving, which he did. Her pussy rippled and clenched along his length as he slid in and out of her, and he slowed the pace as he tried to think of what needed to be done on the ranch so he wouldn't go off too soon. She had him so triggered he couldn't hold back anymore. Just as he started sliding into her harder, deeper, and faster she began rocking her hips to his rhythm and he could feel the tension building inside her. She was as close to climax as he was. Luther lifted his mouth from hers, pushed Jer's hand from her breast, and started sucking on her nipple.

The heat inside her increased and more of her cum coated his cock. Her moaning got louder, the tension in her body built and built as her pussy walls closed in around him. The heat at the base of his spine turned to a flaming inferno and spread around to encompass his balls and cock. The friction of her walls on his dick was so good, it was almost too much.

And then his balls hardened as they drew up closer to his body. Bryant shoved into her one, two, three more times, growling and grunting, and then he was coming. He shouted with rapture as he exploded with her. Her walls contracted and pulsed around his cock, enhancing his peak as cum spurted from his balls up the length of his dick and into the end of the latex.

The orgasm was the longest and most intense he'd ever experienced and he wanted make love to her again and again and again. He'd never be able to get enough of her. He ran his hands over her belly, hips, and legs while trying to regain his breath and stared at the love of his life with awe.

If his brothers hadn't been there with him, Bryant would have told her he loved her, but he wanted to say it the first time in private. He didn't want her to feel like she had to say it back, although from the look in her eyes as she stared at him, she wasn't far behind him with her feelings.

At least that's what he hoped.

* * * *

Jeremiah was so aroused his cock was leaking a constant stream of pre-cum. He loved watching Bryant making love to her but he needed her, too. When she reached out for him and started tugging on his shirt his heart soared. Tori wanted him as well.

He moved around the end of the counter stripping as he went and looked up when he saw Luther doing the same. After he was naked and had on a condom he moved between her legs as Bryant stepped back. He just hoped that he could last and make her come first, or at the same time he did.

"Do you want my cock, honey?"

"Yes. I need you." She tilted her head back and looked at Luther. "I need you both."

Jeremiah smiled and ran his fingers through her soaked folds. He really wanted a taste of her cum, but he was too hungry for her. He planned to lick her pussy and finger fuck her at a later date. Right now he needed to be inside her. After gathering some of her cream onto the tip of his fingers he started rubbing over her clit. Luther braced his hands on the counter and got up with Tori.

He aligned his cock with her pussy and began to push inside.

"I want your mouth on me, baby. Will you suck my cock?" Luther asked as he positioned himself over her. Luther braced his hands and feet lengthwise on the counter so that he was doing a push-up with his cock hovering right above her lips.

Tori didn't answer Luther, at least not verbally. She gripped the base of Luther's cock and pulled it to her mouth.

"Fuck, yes." Luther groaned when Tori swirled her tongue all around Luther's crown and then she sucked him down. "So fucking good."

Jeremiah had been pressing into her the whole time he watched Tori and Luther but he paused when he was inside her to the hilt, giving her time to adjust to his size and penetration. Plus he needed a little time to get his hunger under control. She was so damn tight and he was way too close to shooting off before her.

When he was sure he wasn't about to lose his load, he started moving while he watched Tori giving Luther head. Bryant came back after going to the bathroom to get rid of the condom and moved to the end of the counter. His brother palmed Tori's breast and then Bryant started sucking on her nipple.

Jeremiah started rocking his hips and shoving his cock into her faster. She moaned and slurped around Luther's cock. It was an awesome sight to see his hard-ass brother balancing on his hands and feet, trembling above her while she bobbed up and down over his cock. He was more excited and aroused than he'd ever been and he knew he wouldn't last long.

Being careful not to pull her off of Luther's dick, he gripped her knees and pushed her legs up and back toward her body, and being careful not to push Luther off the counter from his precarious position, and then he started pounding in and out of her. Jeremiah sped up his caressing fingers on her clit and when he felt her inner walls tremble and grip him tighter he knew she was about to go over.

"Baby, I'm gonna come," Luther rasped. "Do you want me to pull out?"

Tori groaned but then she reached up and started rolling Luther's balls in his sac. Luther's whole body tightened, his muscles standing out since they were pumped with blood, and then he shouted as Tori took his cock deeper into her mouth. Her throat worked and she swallowed, breathed in through her nose, and then swallowed again and again as Luther shot down her throat.

Jeremiah and Tori were right on the edge of release, but he waited until Luther pulled from her mouth before sending her over. He shuttled his cock in and out of her rapidly and squeezed her clit between his thumb and index finger. Tori froze as her belly quivered and her legs shook and then she opened her mouth on a scream.

Her cunt flooded with cum and her walls contracted around his gliding dick over and over again. He thrust into her hard and deep, his balls drew up, and then he yelled as he came. Stars exploded before his eyes and he gasped for breath as he was enveloped in a bliss so acute he didn't know how he was still standing. Spume after spume of cum shot up from his balls and out into the tip of his condom. When he came back to himself he realized that his legs were shaking and he'd locked his knees to keep on his feet. With gentle care he lowered Tori's legs back down and lifted her upper body into his arms, hugging her tight. She clung to him, still panting for breath, and when he felt moisture on his shoulder and chest he realized she was crying.

He drew back slightly so he could see her face and became really worried when he saw the tears coursing down her cheeks. "Tori, did I hurt you? God, I'm so sorry, honey."

She sniffled. "You didn't hurt me, Jer. It was just so…"

"Good?" he asked in a whisper.

She shook her head but then nodded. "It was better than good. It was perfect." Tori looked over her shoulder to Luther and then at Bryant. "It was beautiful. Special."

"Yes it was," he replied.

And right then Jeremiah fell head over heels in love with the woman of his dreams.

Chapter Ten

Tori had been so busy serving customers she was glad when there was a lull and leaned against the counter. She watched the newly married Cashmere Morten looking at baby clothes. She'd met Cash and a lot of other women involved in ménage relationships the day of the grand opening, and even though she been asked if she wanted to have a night out with them, she'd been too tired.

Cash giggled when one of her men leaned down and whispered in her ear and swatted him on the stomach. They looked so happy and in love. Tori was just about to go over to see if they wanted some help when she caught movement out the shop window. She began to feel a little scared.

This wasn't the first time she'd seen that guy across the road staring into the shop, but she had thought maybe she was being a little paranoid. He hadn't been there before Cash and Bruce came into the store, but she'd seen him a few times when the shop was being refurbished and when they were setting out all the displays. At first she figured he was just curious about the new store and too shy or intimidated by the baby things and maternity wear to come inside when they'd opened, but she had quickly discarded that scenario. She'd even seen him watching when Trick was working with her but had forgotten to say anything because of the line of customers needing to be served.

But the more she thought about him the more concerned she got. Surely he'd have worked up the courage to come inside by now if he was that curious. A knot of dread formed in the pit of her stomach.

Trick was here today, but he was in the back office going through the software to see what stock needed to be replaced. She wished she could go out there and talk to him, but she wasn't about to leave the shop when there were customers. What frustrated her was that the guy had a hat on his head and it was pulled down low, which put his face in shadows and she couldn't see his face. He kind of looked a little out of shape with his pot belly and she had a feeling he was middle-aged, but she couldn't be sure. She just hoped that if he was trying to gather up the courage to come inside instead of lurking out there, he would.

Pushing him from her mind she hurried over to Cashmere and Bruce. "Do you need some help?"

"Not really," Cash said and glanced at her tall, muscular husband. "We're just looking at the moment."

Tori glanced at Cash's flat stomach and wondered if she'd just found out if she was pregnant. She picked up a little all-in-one baby suit and sighed. "It's so small. I can't wait to have a baby."

"Are congratulations in order?" Tori asked.

Cash gave her a soft, dreamy smile but shook her head. "No. We're still in the practice stage. This is for Shelby Alcott. Her and her husbands, Cord and Brandt, have just found out they're expecting."

"That's wonderful."

"Have you met Shelby?" Cash asked.

"Um…"

Cash smiled. "She has long brown hair and brown eyes and is about five four."

Tori snapped her fingers. "Yes, she was in yesterday buying furniture for the nursery."

"We'll have to arrange for a night out so you can meet everyone. Maybe on Saturday afternoon or Sunday next weekend?"

"I'd love that, thanks."

"Good." Cash led the way to the counter and register with the baby suit in hand and then snatched up one of the teddy bears on the counter to purchase too.

"Your men are invited, too."

Tori nodded and smiled, rang up the sale, and then gave Cash her change.

"We'll have a cookout. Give me your cell number and I'll call you."

After exchanging phone numbers and saying good-bye, Tori watched Cash and Bruce leave. She was glad that the guy who'd been standing outside diagonally across the road was gone and put him from her mind as she started hanging some of the clothes onto racks and thought about last night.

She'd spent the entire night sandwiched between Jeremiah and Luther and hoped to spend many more between her men. It was just over a week since she'd moved in with them and she was so happy. Tori had never thought to find one man right for her, let alone three, but that's what had happened. With every day and night she spent with them she fell more and more in love. It was so nice having someone to come home to, to share her day with and listen to them as they shared with her. There was nowhere else she'd rather be.

Bryant had spent the night before last sleeping with and holding her, and she hoped that she'd never have to be alone again. It hurt to even think about things not working out, so she didn't even go there. Tori knew she was still a little insecure in regards to relationships and hoped she would gain confidence with each passing day. She wanted to tell them she loved them, but none of them had told her that they loved her, and she didn't want to be the one to say it first. The last thing she wanted was Luther, Jeremiah, or Bryant telling her they loved her out of a sense of obligation. She wanted those words to come from their hearts when they were ready.

She already knew that they cared. They'd each said so in their own way, telling her how amazing she was and how special, but she needed to know she was loved, not just liked. Hopefully soon she would hear the words she wanted to hear. It was really hard biting those three words back when they were making love to her, but she had managed to so far.

Last night had blown her mind. Jeremiah had come up to her the moment she'd come of out of the bathroom wrapped in towel fresh from her shower. He'd cupped her face in his hands and then he'd started kissing her. That kiss had been hot and wild from the first meeting of lips and she'd melted against him. Without breaking the kiss he'd lifted her into his arms and carried her to the bed. Her hands had gripped his bare, shirtless shoulders as he'd covered her body with his and then she'd been touching all the warm skin with those steely muscles beneath. She hadn't even heard when Luther and Bryant had come into the room, but she'd felt the mattress dip on either side of her as they got onto the bed.

The towel had been tugged away and then three sets of hands and mouths were kissing and caressing all over her naked body. The passion that had been simmering inside heated up and she'd groaned with frustration when Jer had broken the kiss.

"You're so fucking passionate, honey." Jer kissed his way down her chest, over her belly until he was between her spread thighs and his mouth a hairbreadth away from her pussy. "I'll never get enough of you Tori."

And then his mouth had been on her cunt, lapping and laving at her clit as he pushed a finger up inside her creating that exquisite friction that sent her on a path to the stars. Warmth had filled her heart and those three words were on the tip of her tongue, but she swallowed them back down. Just as she thought she was about to go over the edge, Jeremiah had stopped and had turned her onto her side.

His hands had rubbed over and then gripped and kneaded her ass cheeks. "I love this ass. Will you let me fuck it? Will you let all of us make love with you?"

Tori wanted that so much. She wanted them all inside her appeasing the deep ache. She wanted them loving her until she screamed their names.

"Yes," her answer came out on a moan.

She heard the pop of a bottle and then cold wet fingers were rubbing over her ass. She whimpered and pushed her bottom back into Jeremiah's touch. When his finger breached her anus she began to tremble with desire and reached out to Luther.

Luther slanted his mouth over hers again and again and again. By the time the carnal kiss ended Jer had three fingers in her rectum stretching her out. Her pussy clenched on emptiness and cream wept onto her thighs. Bryant was plucking and sucking at her breasts driving her insane with need.

And then Jer was pushing his lubed-up, condom-covered cock into her ass. She gasped with pleasure at the dark carnality of having a dick in her rear entrance. When he was inside her all the way, he gripped her hips firmly and then lifted her leg and pulled it back over the top of his thigh.

Luther released her mouth, aligned his body with hers, and eased his latex-covered rod into her pussy. How the two men managed to lift and turn taking her with them she had no idea. But a moment later Jeremiah was underneath her, his cock still inside her anus and Luther was on top of her. And then they moved her again so that she was sitting on Luther's thighs with Jer behind her.

Bryant got up onto his knees and stroked her cheek with the head of his dick. Tori wrapped her hand around the base of his shaft and brought it to her mouth. She'd sucked and licked, pleased with the grunts and growls he'd made as she'd given him head.

Jer and Luther had started sliding their cocks in and out of her ass and pussy sending her on the long, slow, pleasurable climb toward nirvana. Tori had felt so full of love, so full of emotion, she'd closed her eyes so that Luther and Bryant hadn't seen the tears in her eyes. The yearning to tell them how much they meant to her would have spilled out onto her lips if her mouth hadn't been full of Bryant's cock.

Then he'd warned her he was about to come. She had concentrated on sending him over. He'd come with a yell and she swallowed down his salty-sweet essence until he'd finally withdrawn from her mouth and slumped down onto the bed.

Tori had come next with a soft scream, the pleasure so intense more tears had formed behind her eyes, but she'd held them back barely. But the warmth and love in her heart had been so penetrating, so powerful, she felt consumed by it.

Luther had shouted and met her gaze just as he'd reached his own peak and his eyes had been full of emotions she wasn't sure she could or wanted to identify as yet. Jer had pumped his hard cock into her ass twice more and he too yelled as he climaxed.

She felt so safe and secure in their arms, surrounded by their bodies and heat. She never wanted to be apart from them. She was so deeply in love with them and felt connected to all of them. Her heart stuttered and her belly flipped. Tori had closed her eyes to the intensity of all those feelings and slumped against Luther as she tried to get her breathing back under control, her pussy still quaking with aftershocks.

And then she had fallen asleep in their arms.

She jerked when Trick called out to her as he came in from the back of the store, pulling her from her introspection. "There's a problem at the bank I have to go sort out. Will you be okay by yourself for a while?"

"Sure, I think everyone's having lunch." Tori glanced at her watch to see that it was already 1:30 p.m. and her stomach growled in protest. Trick must have heard because he smiled at her. "Do you want me to bring you something for lunch?"

"No, thanks anyway. I brought a sandwich."

"I hope I won't be too long, but I won't know until I know what the problem is. Call me if you need me." Trick opened the door and waved before leaving.

Tori rushed to the small kitchen, got her sandwich from the fridge and a bottle of water, and headed back to the counter to eat. Just as she finished and put her lunch wrap in the trash the door opened. She stood up, and her hands went clammy as the man who'd been observing the store walked toward her.

He stopped in front of her and stared down at her. She'd been right. The guy had to be in his late forties or early fifties.

"Can I help you?"

"Yes," he replied but continued to stare at her.

Tori was getting really scared now and slowly edged toward the phone at the other end of the counter.

"What can I help you with?"

"Well, now, there a lot of things, but the only thing I'm interested in is getting back at Trick Wendall."

Tori's legs started shaking and her face felt like all the blood had drained from it, but she tried to keep her expression stoic.

"I can call Mr. Wendall to come and see you." Tori picked up the phone receiver but squeaked with fright when his hand covered hers and stopped her from lifting it to her ear. His grip was hard and it felt like he was going to break the bones in her hand and fingers. She stared at him, not sure what to do or say, and after a moment he changed his grip from her hand to her wrist and pried the phone from her clasp, before placing it back in the cradle.

He pulled her with him as he walked to the end of the counter and she whimpered when her hip kept hitting the edge. She was going to end up with a bruise over her hipbone, because he wasn't even trying to be gentle.

"Look, Mr.—"

"We'll wait until we're on our way before I introduce myself." The man tugged her out from behind the counter and then pulled her toward the hallway in the back.

Tori dug her heels in, but he was much bigger and stronger than her and she didn't even seem to slow him down.

"I don't know what Trick's done to upset you, but I had nothing to do with it. Please, let me go."

"Shut up. Do you think I don't know you're his girlfriend? He ruined my life and it's time he knows what that feels like."

Tori gulped when she realized he was dragging her to the back door. If he managed to get her from the store there was no telling what he would end up doing to her. Her heart was racing so hard in her chest it was a wonder it hadn't exploded. She couldn't seem to get enough air into her lungs and she was shaking like a leaf, but she knew she had to keep him talking. If she distracted him enough she may just be able to get away from him.

But before she could think of anything to say he had her outside and was heading toward the truck parked in the loading bay behind the shop. Tori hit out at him, but he must have seen it coming. He spun around, grabbed her fist in his large hand, and squeezed hard as he pushed her down to her knees.

"You're not going to get away, you little bitch. You and your boyfriend need to suffer just like I have. That fucker ruined my marriage and made me lose my farm. Now he needs to know what it's like to lose someone important to him."

Tori could see the fury in his eyes as he snarled at her. Spittle flew from his mouth and hit her cheek, making her gag. She tried to get to her feet, but with him holding her wrist in one hand and her fist in the other while he applied bruising pressure, she didn't stand a chance.

When she was able to get one foot flat on the ground he let go of her fist and grabbed her hair so hard she cried out as strands pulled from her head. He released her wrist and started dragging her across the concrete on her knees. Tori's skin scraped and started burning as he pulled her along behind him. She grabbed at his wrist and dug her nails into his skin as hard as she could and then yelled when the back of his hand connected with her cheek. She hadn't even seen him turn back toward her so she hadn't been able to block the blow. Her cheek throbbed, but she continued fighting him. She wasn't about to give up until she got away.

She hadn't even had the chance to tell Luther, Jeremiah, and Bryant she loved them. Tears spilled from her eyes and onto her cheeks and her knees felt like they were being torn to shreds, but she was going to get away from him.

He hauled her to her feet by her hair and then shoved her into the truck. Her breast and shoulder connected with the metal frame and she screamed with pain. Her ass landed on the seat, but when he went to grab her ankles she kicked out at him. He grunted when her foot landed in his solar plexus and she lifted her other foot to kick him again.

Agony assailed her ankle and leg when he twisted it hard and wrenched it, snapping the bone just above her ankle and all she could do was moan as agony assailed her. The pain was too much for her to even cry out and she couldn't even breathe.

He shoved her legs into the truck and slammed the door behind him. Tori was hurting so bad she felt sick to her stomach, but she couldn't give up. She watched him through blurry eyes as he walked around the truck toward the driver's seat and she pulled at the door handle. It wouldn't budge. She straightened in her seat and hugged the door, staying as far away from him as possible, and tried to calm her breathing to circumvent the nausea roiling in her gut. Her head and heart were pounding and her ankle, foot, and lower leg were throbbing with every beat of her heart and every breath she took.

He got into the truck, gave her an evil look, and then turned the key. He drove out of the back access lane and headed out of Slick Rock. Tori looked around to see if anyone saw them, but he'd kept away from the main road and the streets he traveled were empty.

Her only hope was that Trick came back to the shop and found her gone.

* * * *

Luther stretched out his aching back as he watched the cattle investigating their new home. Their stock was good quality and they had calves, heifers, and two bulls. Hopefully by next spring every one of those cows would be ready to drop another calf. Just as he finished checking the automatic watering trough to make sure it was working properly, his cell rang.

He glanced at the screen and didn't recognize the number and was about to put it back in his pocket, but he decided to see who was calling. They were expecting a delivery of seed for planting in the far pasture and since it hadn't been delivered yet, he thought the company might be trying to contact him.

"Luther Katz."

"Luther, it's Trick Wendall."

"Wendall," Luther said. "What's up?"

"Is Tori there?"

Luther's whole body went on alert. He could hear concern in Trick's voice and it was strange that Wendall was calling him looking for Tori when she was at the shop.

"What the hell kind of game are you playing, Wendall? You know damn well that Tori's with you."

Jeremiah and Bryant looked up from the fence they'd just finished fixing and walked over to him with frowns on their faces.

"I'm not playing any games," Trick snapped. "Just answer the fucking question. Is. Tori. There?"

"No."

"Fuck."

Luther's heart flipped in his chest and then started pounding. He pushed the speakerphone button and turned the volume up so his brothers could hear Trick.

"Tori's missing."

"What?" Luther roared and started rushing toward his truck.

"I had to leave and fix a problem at the bank. I was gone no more than twenty minutes. When I got back the shop was still wide open and Tori was gone."

"Is her car there?" Luther asked as he got into the driver's seat. Jeremiah and Bryant got into the truck, too.

"Yes and so is her bag."

"Shit."

"I've called Luke and informed him that she's missing."

"Who the hell would want to hurt Tori?" Jeremiah yelled his question.

"I don't know. Hopefully when Luke and Damon get here we can work it out."

"We'll be there in ten minutes." Luther tossed his phone to Jeremiah and planted his foot on the accelerator. Gravel sprayed up from under the tires and the truck fishtailed down the drive.

He hardly slowed down as he turned onto the road and then pushed the pedal to the floor. Just as he was picking up speed, a truck came toward them from the opposite direction. He glanced over and blanched when he saw Tori in the passenger seat of the truck with an older man behind the wheel.

Luther tugged on the handbrake and the truck spun around. After releasing the brake he put his foot back on the accelerator. "Call Luke and give him the license plate. He can run a check and see who has taken Tori."

Jeremiah dialed and started talking, but Luther didn't bother listening in. He was hell-bent on catching up with that asshole and getting the love of his life back. He hadn't even told her how he felt and now he may never get the chance.

No, that asshole's not going to win. I need her more than my next breath.

He pushed the pedal harder and so did the guy driving the truck in front of him. The fucker swerved to the other side of the road and Luther was able to get closer. That's when he saw that Tori was fighting him. He held his breath until the guy got the truck back under control and then he roared with fury when he saw the bastard hit his woman.

"Get closer, Luther," Bryant demanded.

Luther glanced in the rearview mirror just as Bryant opened the back window, pushed his head and upper body through, and then climbed out into the bed of the truck. They all had rifles, but there was no way they were shooting at that motherfucker. The last thing Luther wanted was for Tori to get shot.

Luther glanced at the road ahead and was pleased that the road was straight and clear for now. He maneuvered the truck to the other side of the road and pressed harder on the accelerator pedal. He'd never been so glad in his life that his truck was the latest model. It was bigger and had more power than the one Tori was in.

He pulled the truck alongside the older one and Jeremiah lowered the window.

"Pull over!" Jeremiah yelled.

Luther frowned when he saw the man's face and tried to remember where he'd seen him before, but he couldn't. His anxiety was through the roof with fear for Tori and he couldn't seem to think straight.

Jeremiah lifted the rifle from his lap and pointed it at the other truck. Luther knew his brother was just trying to scare the asshole into stopping and wouldn't shoot but the other guy didn't know that.

Or maybe he did.

Luther cursed when the bastard gave them an evil smile before facing the road again. He looked in the mirror and saw Bryant was on the opposite side of the bed and he moved the truck close to the other one. After making sure the road was still clear he edged over until there was no more than a couple of feet between the vehicles. Bryant was going to have to move fast because there was a curve coming up and it was too dangerous for him to stay on the wrong side of the road.

Bryant jumped and Luther hit the brakes. When he was far enough away from the other vehicle he pulled back in behind him and just in the nick of time. A semitruck came barreling around the curve.

"That was fucking close, man," Jeremiah said.

Luther nodded but kept his eye on Bryant and Tori. Bryant was gripping the roll bar to the back of and above the other truck's cab but his body was turned side-on so Luther could see his mouth moving. He wondered if he was trying to talk the fucker into stopping or giving Tori instructions.

Bryant bent over at the waist and when he stood up again he had a crowbar in his hand and then he swung it at the back window. Luther hoped like hell that none of that glass cut Tori, but it was imperative that they rescue her.

When the glass was gone Bryant reached in and placed his hand on the fucker's neck. Tori moved and placed her hand on the steering wheel. Luther sighed with relief when he saw the bastard slump against the driver's door, but the truck started picking up speed. The unconscious man must have still had his foot on the accelerator. Bryant bent down until his head and chest were inside the cab and then he pulled the man out through the back window. As the truck slowed, Tori steered it with one hand until it finally came to a stop on the grass verge.

Luther pulled in behind the other truck and was out of the vehicle moments later. He ran to the passenger door, but Bryant was already there. His brother was already reaching in for Tori, but she drew back, flinched, and moaned as if she was in a lot of pain.

"Tori, are you all right, darlin'?"

Tori took the hand Bryant offered but didn't move to get out of the truck. Luther leaned around Bryant and sucked in a breath when he saw her bruised cheek and jaw. He turned when Jeremiah came up behind him. "Call the paramedics."

"I'm okay," Tori said in a wobbly voice.

"Baby, you're hurt."

She looked at him through tear-filled eyes and gave a little sob. She was breaking his heart. Luther needed to hold her in his arms and make sure that she was okay. He nudged Bryant aside and pushed his arm beneath her knees.

"I think my ankle is broken."

Luther carefully lifted her from the cab and carried her toward his truck. Jeremiah rushed ahead of him and opened the back door.

"I was so scared, baby," Luther said and he gently lowered her to the backseat. "We had no idea what had happened to you and didn't know where to start looking."

"I don't even know that guy." Tori sucked in a breath and gripped his hand. "I think he thought that Trick and I were...involved."

Tori started crying and Luther hated seeing see her so upset and in so much pain. He glanced down the road when he heard the siren and saw the sheriff had arrived.

"Don't talk, baby, just try and rest."

Trick jumped out of the back of the sheriff's truck and ran over to them. He glanced into the back of the other vehicle and paled. "Fuck."

Luke Sun-Walker and Damon Osborne, the two sheriffs, walked over.

"You know that guy?" Bryant asked in a cold voice.

"Yeah." Trick scrubbed a hand over his face. "He came into the bank a couple of months back and asked for a loan. I had to refuse. He was already mortgaged to the hilt and had missed six months' worth of payments.

"His wife left three months ago and he came back to beg me for more time before the bank foreclosed on his property."

"Goddamn it, Wendall."

"Look," Trick said. "I know you blame me for what's happened, but I tried to help him twelve months ago. But he was too fucking stubborn to listen. It didn't matter what I did or said. Marcus White was on the path to destruction and there wasn't a damn thing I could do about it."

Just as Trick finished explaining, Marcus groaned and came to. Luke and Damon hauled him out of the back of the truck, handcuffed him, and read him his rights.

"I'm sorry you got hurt because of me, Tori."

"It wasn't your fault," Tori whispered. Luther didn't like seeing her in so much pain and wanted to push Wendall back, but his woman seemed determined to alleviate Trick's guilt. "You aren't responsible for what other people say or what they do. There's nothing to forgive."

"Thank you, Tori. Now you let your men take good care of you. You need to go and see the doctor."

"Yes, I do. I hope you advertised for employees."

"I did."

"That's good because I don't think I'm going to be back at work for quite a while. That bastard broke my ankle."

Trick looked horrified and his faced paled even more if that were possible. He apologized again and then followed Luke and Damon back to the sheriff's truck.

"You take as long as you need to heal, Tori. I have the shop covered."

"Let's get you some medical help, baby." Luther got into the driver's seat and Jeremiah got into the back with Tori. Bryant sat up front with him.

Moments later they were headed back to Slick Rock. Luther cursed under his breath every time the truck went over a bump and he saw Tori wince. He should have demanded that the paramedics be sent out, but she could be so stubborn sometimes. She was like him in a lot of respects but way better looking and a lot softer and sweeter than he'd ever be.

"Try and relax, honey." Jeremiah was supporting Tori's upper body and cuddling her close. "God, Tori, you scared the shit out of us. We had no idea what was going on or where to look."

"I know," Tori said through gritted teeth and then winced in pain. "I think that man thought Trick and I were involved romantically as well as business partners. He said he wanted to take something away from Trick that he cared for. I don't even know why he thought that.

We don't see each other that way. It's more like a brother-sister relationship."

The worry about her working with Trick eased from Luther's heart. Even though she'd told them she wasn't attracted to Wendall he'd still been a little trepidatious. He'd seen the attraction in the Wendall brothers' eyes when she'd first introduced them. But he'd been worried over nothing. Tori was theirs and no one was taking her away from them. He had plans and nothing would stop him until he got what he wanted.

Tori in their lives forever.

"He saw what he wanted to see, baby," Luther said and glanced in the mirror. "That man was blaming everyone for his circumstances but himself. Maybe if he had taken Trick up on his offer for help a year ago he might have been able to save his marriage and his home. He'll pay the price for his actions now."

Luther heard her gasp as the truck went over a bump, so he slowed his speed to below the maximum limit and avoided all the bumps he could, but by the time they got to the clinic Luther was sweating buckets. Tori looked so helpless and fragile. He wanted to go to the sheriff's office and grab that bastard by the throat and break a few of his bones and see how he liked it.

After pulling into the parking lot of the doctor's office he jumped out of the truck and opened the back door. Between him, Jeremiah, and Bryant, they had Tori in the clinic seeing the doctor.

After she was checked over for other injuries and X-rayed, the doc plastered her right leg from her toes to just below her knee and the pain medication was kicking in. Thankfully, as they drove back home, Tori fell asleep.

He and his brothers were going to take good care of her while she healed. There was no way they were leaving her alone ever again.

Chapter Eleven

It had been three weeks since Tori had been abducted by Marcus White, and even though she was grateful for the care her men had given her, she was starting to go stir crazy. At least one of her men was with her all the time, and no matter how much she argued with them that she was fine to be left alone, they wouldn't hear it.

At first the crutches had been difficult to get the hang of, but she had after a few days, and she'd told Luther that he could go out and work with his brothers.

"Not happening, baby." Luther crossed his arms over his chest and stared down at her with an implacable resolve.

"Luther…"

"No." He knelt down at her feet, took her face between his hands, and stared into her eyes. "I couldn't stand it if you fell and hurt yourself and one of us wasn't here to help you."

"But…"

"We nearly fucking lost you, Tori. I never want to go through anything like that ever again."

Before she'd had time to reply he'd kissed her softly on the lips and then headed into the kitchen to make some lunch.

Of course Tori hadn't stayed put. She got to her feet with her crutches under her arms intending to help him get lunch. She'd been so intent on trying to work the damn things she hadn't heard Luther come back in.

"What the hell…"

Tori wobbled and looked up and when she felt herself falling she cried out. Luther rushed over and lifted her from her feet, the crutches falling to the floor with a loud clatter.

"I told you…"

"If you hadn't scared the shit out of me I would have been fine," Tori said scathingly. "I swear you and your brothers must have lived with cougars or something."

Luther chuckled, kissed on her on the forehead, and then carried her back to the sofa, but instead of putting her down on the cushion he sat down, plonked her in his lap, and started kissing her. Tori moaned as she lost herself in his taste, in his and her own passion. By the time he'd lifted his head her anger was gone and she'd wanted to make love with him, but of course he'd refused.

"Take me to bed." Tori pushed her hand up under his shirt caressing his chest and abs.

"Not happening, baby. You're still in pain and there is no way in hell I'm going to add to it by making love with you and accidentally hurting your ankle."

When she'd opened her mouth to protest he'd just kissed her again. The rest of the afternoon was spent watching movies and kissing. By then end of the day her panties were soaked through.

Jeremiah had been just as bad. He'd caught her making her way toward the verandah out back and before she could say a word he'd scooped her up into his arms, crutches and all, and carried her back to the sofa.

"The next time you want to go somewhere, you call me first. Understand?"

Tori hadn't answered. She just glared at him. The stare down seemed to last forever but finally she'd looked away and when she'd heard him chuckling under his breath in what sounded like victory, she'd wanted to hit him, but he'd already been walking away.

"Bastard," she muttered.

"I heard that," Jer called out and peeked around the corner of the door. Tori flipped him off.

Bryant was the same as his brothers only in a completely different way. He got her things like drink and food before she even asked for them, not giving her the chance to even get up off the sofa. And when she did to go to the bathroom he followed behind her holding her hips in case she fell. When he'd gone to follow her into the room she turned and looked at him over her shoulder.

"I can take it from here. I don't need your help to use the toilet." Tori had glared at him and he'd given her a grin and held his hands palm out in a placating gesture.

Although she still had the crutches she was allowed to walk on her right leg now with their aid and apart from the occasional ache she wasn't experiencing much pain at all. She wanted to go back to work and had actually called Trick to get him to help her talk her men into letting her out, but he'd been in agreement with the Katz brothers and told her she wasn't coming back until the plaster cast was off. Everywhere she turned she was being thwarted and her libido was so primed just a touch of their hand on hers, or on her shoulder, or her back, or her ass was nearly enough to make her orgasm. Luther, Jeremiah, and Bryant touched her constantly and she was in a continuous state of arousal, and she was bored out of her brains. They wouldn't let her do anything besides go to the bathroom or take a bath. And even then she wasn't left totally alone. They hovered outside the bathroom door while she used the facilities and she was never alone when she bathed. In fact they helped to wash her and that only made matters worse.

There was only so much a woman could take and Tori was at the end of her rope. If she didn't get relief soon she may just do or say something she would regret, and she didn't want that. Even happy-go-lucky, easygoing Bryant had been on her case about resting and wouldn't let her hobble into the kitchen for a drink. Something had to give, and she had a feeling it was going to be her.

Felicity had visited and after arranging a cookout to be held at the Katz brothers' ranch she and the other women along with their men had turned up bringing all the salads and dessert so that all Luther, Jeremiah, and Bryant needed to do was supply and grill the meat.

"You look like you're ready to scream." Felicity smirked at her.

Tori explained how her men had been treating her like she was about to break.

"I know what that feels like." Shelby patted Tori's hand. "My men were the same after getting me out of that cave." Shelby went on to explain how she'd witnessed the murder of her family and how the perpetrator had escaped and come after her.

"Oh my God," Tori whispered and covered her mouth with her hand as she glanced over to the grill where all the men were talking as they stood around the cooking meat, while they sipped on beers.

"I'm fine," Shelby reassured her. "That asshole got his just desserts when the cave in killed him."

"Thank God."

"You need to take matters into your own hands," Felicity said as she lifted Carly Rose into her arms when she came over after being with her daddies.

"What do you mean?" Tori asked.

"Do you have any sexy lingerie?" Shelby asked with a sly smile.

"No."

"I think it's time we went shopping," Flick said.

"They're not going to let me out without one of them with me."

"No. Bast…darn." Shelby glanced at Carly Rose.

"We can go for her," Felicity suggested. "We can find something a little less appropriate and drop it in."

"You don't need clothes to seduce men," Cash said.

"She's right. I have a better idea," Shelby said and then glanced at Carly Rose again.

"Carly go and give you Daddies a nice big hug and kiss."

"'Kay, Mommy." Carly Rose slid to the ground and tottered over to her fathers.

Tori listened avidly as Shelby gave her suggestions to seduce her men, and Cash and Felicity added a few of their own. By the time the food was ready to eat, all four of them had pink cheeks and were squirming in their seats. Tori hugged all three women. "You three are the best. Thanks. I'll give them a few more days but if they continue to ignore my signals then I'll make my move."

Shelby giggled. "Those three men are going down."

"They don't stand a chance," Felicity smiled.

Tori tapped each lady's glass of ice tea with her own. "To victory."

"To victory," Cash, Shelby, and Felicity echoed.

That had been four days ago, and besides her men she hadn't seen another adult. But what was even worse was that she never got to spend any time alone. Even though she loved spending time with her men, she needed the occasional downtime from them, too. She couldn't see that happening for another three weeks, which was when she would finally be able to get the pesky, itchy plaster cast off.

Luther was currently in the kitchen heating up the casserole that Cash had brought over the day of the cookout. All the women had brought over dishes that had been frozen and only needed to be defrosted and heated before they were ready to eat. Tori was glad about that, because although her men could cook, their food repertoire was limited to steak and salad and steak and vegetables. There was only so much steak a girl could eat before she started craving chicken or pasta and other things.

The weather was also warming up as they headed from spring to summer, and Luther had been walking around the house all day without a shirt on. She loved seeing his body and watching the way his muscles moved beneath the skin on his broad shoulders and wide chest, but it also had her in a constant state of arousal. She couldn't take any more of their unconscious teasing. Her panties were soaked through and her cut-off jean shorts weren't far behind. She just hadn't figured out what to do about the situation. No, that wasn't true. She just needed to shore up her courage to put her plan into action. She needed a little bolstering from her friends.

Glancing toward the kitchen door, she heard Luther start chopping the vegetables for the salad that would accompany the casserole and decided it was safe to get a little advice. She and Shelby had really clicked at the cookout and now they were really good friends, too. Tori checked to make sure her phone was on silent and then sent Shelby a text message.

It's been three weeks since we've had sex and I'm about ready to pop. I'm not sure if I can do what we talked about.

LOL. You poor thing. Sure you can. You're a sexy confident woman and they want you as much as you want them. I could see it in their eyes every time they looked at you. What you need to do is...

Tori covered her mouth to muffle her snicker and then sent a thank-you to Shelby planning to catch up with her soon.

If Jeremiah and Bryant were running on schedule then they should be home in about five minutes. Perfect.

Tori lowered the crutches leaning on the sofa next to her and stood up. She glanced toward the kitchen again and heard that Luther was still chopping. *Thank you, God.* She lifted her shirt up over her head and flung it behind the sofa, undid her bra and flung it away, too. After releasing the button on her shorts, she pushed them and her panties over her hips and sat down on the couch. Getting the shorts off over her left leg was easy, but getting them and her panties off over her right was a little harder because of the cast. She managed without wriggling around too much, or making too much noise.

Now that she was totally naked she arranged herself on the sofa so that the first thing Jeremiah and Bryant saw when they came inside was her pussy. She placed her upper back against the arm of the sofa, draped her left leg up over the back of it, and then placed the foot of her right casted foot on the floor. She raised one arm over her head and the other she placed on her belly and looked down at herself.

No, not quite right. She moved the arm she had up over her head and cupped her breast with it and then put the other hand on her pussy. She was just in time. She could hear Jeremiah and Bryant walking up the porch's timber steps and then they were at the door.

The door opened and she heard their boots hit the floor in the entry. Tori closed her eyes, started massaging her breast and fingering her pussy, and she moaned. And as she lay there playing with herself, hoping that the sight of what she was doing would be enough to entice her men into breaking their control and making love with her, she realized that she hadn't told them how she felt about them.

She was going to tell them she loved them, if she got out of her predicament with Marcus, but the pain she'd been in had been too intense and then she'd been on some pretty strong painkillers for a few days. Also she'd been frustrated with having permanent babysitters, and they'd been so authoritative it hadn't been the right time. But it was now.

She rubbed a finger over her clit and moaned out loud just as the footsteps entered the living room.

"Holy shit," Bryant gasped.

"Sweet momma in heaven." Jeremiah groaned.

Tori opened her eyes to slits as she heard Luther rushing from the kitchen to see what was going on, and Tori took that moment to push two fingers up inside her cunt.

"Have mercy, baby."

Tori met each of their eyes as she continued to finger fuck herself and then she looked back at Luther.

"I love you," she panted and then met Jeremiah's eyes again.

"I love you."

She looked at Bryant. "I love you."

They looked shocked for a moment and then the brothers moved to stand side by side at the end of the sofa so she could see them all at once. "I love you all so much. I need you to make love to me."

Luther was the first to react. A slow smile spread across his face. That smile only made him more handsome and her breath caught in her throat. He moved to stand in front of her and then knelt down at her side.

"I love you, too, baby." He bent down and placed the sweetest emotion-filled kiss on her lips and it brought tears to her eyes.

Jeremiah came and knelt beside Luther and shoved his brother out of the way. "I love you, Tori, so damn much." And then he kissed her, but his kiss was hot, wild, and passionate. When he lifted his head she saw Luther heading toward the kitchen and even though she was elated that he loved her, too, she was disappointed because it didn't look like her plan was going to work.

Bryant rushed over to her side, but instead of kneeling down, he bent down and scooped her up into his arms, sitting back down with her on his lap. He rested his forehead against hers and looked deeply into her eyes. "I love you, Tori Springer. You aren't ever getting away from us."

Tori reached up and cupped his cheek. "I don't want to."

"That's good, darlin', because we plan to spend the rest of our lives taking care of and loving you." He didn't give her a chance to say anything else because his mouth covered hers.

While he was kissing her, he rose to his feet and then he was walking down toward the bedroom. She worried that Luther wasn't there, but then she heard two sets of footsteps following behind and relaxed. It looked like the advice Shelby had given her had worked after all.

Bryant lowered her to the bed and followed her down. He kissed her hungrily and she kissed him just as rapaciously, but she groaned with frustration when he broke the kiss and got off the bed. She was about to demand that they make love to her, but the words froze on her lips when her three men began to quickly shuck their clothes.

Jeremiah was the fastest, and once he was naked he crawled up on the bed between her legs, pushed them further apart, and then he was licking her cunt. She arched up and whimpered as his tongue slid over her folds and then lapped over her clit. He flicked the sensitive bundle of nerves a few times and then he moved back down to her hole and started fucking his tongue in and out of her. The sensation was so good, it was like warm, moist velvet caressing her inner walls and it had her on the verge of a climax in seconds, but then he stopped when Luther and Jeremiah got on the bed with them.

"We all want to make love to you at the same time, honey, and if you agree we'll need to prepare your ass so we don't hurt you. Will you let us, Tori? Do you trust us not to hurt you?"

"I trust you. With my life, my heart, and my soul. You've all made love to me together before and didn't hurt me. Why are you worried you will now?"

"We aren't worried, darlin'," Bryant replied. "We just want to make sure you want this, too. We know sometimes you won't want all of us together."

"Plus we are always going to make you know what we are going to do to you. That way there are no surprises," Luther said.

"I love surprises."

"God, I love you." Jeremiah kissed her belly and then she was being turned over onto her stomach.

"I love you all, too." Her voice was muffled by the pillow until she turned her head to the side.

Luther lay down next to her and then he was kissing her. The kiss was hot, wild, wet, and carnal. He nipped and sucked and licked until they were both breathless.

"I want you to stay nice and relaxed for me, honey. Try not to tense up," Jeremiah rasped.

Tori nodded and closed her eyes. She heard the pop of a bottle and knew what was coming. Although she was a little trepidatious since she'd only had anal sex once before, she was also very eager. She wanted to have the physical connection of them all making love to her as well as the emotional one that she felt with each of them.

She took a deep breath as her ass cheeks were separated and relaxed all her muscles as she exhaled. And then Jeremiah's fingers were caressing the skin of her rosette. It felt so good, she wanted more and pushed her ass into his touch.

"Don't move, darlin'," Bryant whispered into her ear and then kissed her shoulder. "Just relax and let us do all the work."

Jeremiah took his time getting her used to his touch in such an unusual place, and the more he touched her the more turned on she became. One finger penetrated her anus and then two. She loved the slight burning, pinching pain and wanted more. Her pussy clenched and dripped cream and her clit was throbbing along with every beat of her heart as if it was a live entity, too. Her body was one big massive sexual ache, and only the three men she loved with her whole heart could appease it.

"Three fingers now, honey. If the burning gets too much use your muscles and try to push them out. It'll make it easier to get them inside your pretty little bottom."

Just his words were enough to send her up the peak, closer to the edge, and by the time he had three fingers pumping in and out of her ass and stretching her muscles out, she was on the precipice.

"She's close," Jeremiah whispered as he withdrew his fingers from her rosette and he moved aside, cleaning his hand on a wipe.

She heard the rip of a foil pack and then the lube bottle popping open again and then the mattress dipped between her thighs. Luther blanketed her body from behind, his chest hair tickling her back as he wrapped an arm around her waist and lifted her to her hands and knees.

"Are you ready for me, baby?"

"Yes. Now."

"Good girl." Luther began to push the head of his cock into her anus and they both groaned when it popped through the tight muscles. He held still and waited for her to stop clenching on him, giving her a chance to get used to him being inside her. And then he pressed forward another inch and waited. He repeated the advance and pause until he was all the way inside her ass.

Tori couldn't stop whimpering. She'd never felt anything so good in her life and she knew it was only going to get better. This is how she wanted to make love with her men all the time. All three of them touching her, kissing her, and inside of her. Luther lowered his arm to her hips, tightened his grip, and then he carefully got off the bed.

"What…"

"Shh, darlin'," Bryant rasped as he moved in front of her. "We're just trying to make you more comfortable."

Luther straddled the backless sofa near the end of the bed and gently lowered her onto his lap. She mewled as his big hard cock slid in a little deeper. Bryant also straddled the bench and then he held her face between his hands and he kissed her hungrily. When he lifted his head he looked deeply into her eyes.

"I need you, darlin'."

"I need you, too."

Bryant kept his gaze connected with hers and, after rolling on the latex sheath, aimed his cock at her hole and began to push in.

"Fucking perfect," he groaned as he gently rocked his hips forward and back until he was inside her balls-deep. "How are you feeling, Tori?"

"So good. I need more." Tori turned her head when she saw movement from the corner of her eye and looked at Jeremiah as he stepped closer to her. With him standing at her side he was at the perfect height for her to suck his cock.

Tori looked him in the eye and crooked her finger. He smiled at her and did what she wanted. She gripped the base of his cock with her hand and brought him to her mouth. She moaned as the flavor of his pre-cum coated her taste buds and she craved more. After relaxing her jaw she opened her mouth wide and sucked him in.

"Shit, your mouth is heaven. That's it, suck me, honey."

Tori hummed around his cock, letting him know without words how much she loved having him in her mouth, and then she groaned when Luther and Bryant started to move. Luther pulled out, and as he slowly pushed back into her ass, Bryant withdrew from her pussy until just the tip of his cock was inside her hole.

With every rock of their hips they increased the pace until their cocks were shuttling in and out, in and out of her cunt and anus, while she bobbed up and down over Jeremiah's cock. The heat that had been smoldering inside her for the last couple of weeks flared up to a raging conflagration, and the faster they moved the faster she sucked Jeremiah, and the faster she flew up the slope of arousal.

Copious juices coated the inside of her walls and dripped from her pussy, making the slide and glide of Bryant's cock so much easier and the friction built and built until she was being consumed by it.

Jeremiah groaned and his cock jerked in her mouth and she knew he was close to his peak, so she reached out, cupped his balls, and then gently squeezed. "Tori, I'm gonna come, honey. You need to pull off if you don't want a mouthful."

Tori didn't want that. She wanted to taste his essence so she rolled his balls and then squeezed again as she took him in as far as she could and undulated her tongue on the sensitive underside. The grip he had on her hair tightened and then he shouted as his cock expanded and then shot load after load of cum over her tongue and down her throat. She swallowed quickly and savored the spicy flavor of his semen until he had nothing left to give and gently withdrew from her mouth. He sank down to his knees beside her, panting for breath.

Just as she reached out to grip Bryant's arms the fire building inside her engulfed her in their erotic, carnal flames. She screamed as her internal muscles clenched and released, clamped down and let go, with the euphoric waves of climax. She came so hard her whole body shook and shivered. Cream gushed from her pussy, covering her and Bryant as she saw stars.

"Fuck yes," Bryant gasped. "Cover me with your cum, darlin'." And then he shoved into her twice more, yelling the whole time, and then he froze as he, too, reached his peak. The jerking and twitching of his cock drew her orgasm out and enhanced her pleasure so much she thought she was going to pass out.

Luther's hands tightened on her hips and then he, too, roared as he began to orgasm. Tori could feel his body shaking against hers and his hips jerked as his cock shot rope after rope of cum into the end of the condom.

Tori slumped against Bryant, too satiated and boneless to hold herself up as she tried to get her breathing back to normal. Three sets of hands ran all over her body and Jeremiah kissed her knee. When Luther eased his softening cock from her ass, they both groaned and then Bryant carefully withdrew from her pussy. Jeremiah stood up, lifted her into his arms, and carried her into the bathroom.

She luxuriated in their care as they wrapped her cast in plastic and then washed her in the tub. When she was clean and dried off, Luther helped her into a robe, and then she was carried to the kitchen by Bryant. He cuddled her on his lap as Jeremiah and Luther served their dinner. They chatted about their day while eating and then Jeremiah carried her to the living room while Bryant and Luther cleaned up.

She snuggled with Jeremiah and tried to keep her eyes open, but after being loved so well by her men she was struggling to stay awake. Bryant and Luther came in and they sat on either side of her and Jeremiah.

Jeremiah stood up, taking her with him. He placed her on the sofa cushion and he knelt down with both his hands resting on her thighs. Luther cleared his throat and took one of her hands in his.

"I love you, Tori Springer. Will you marry me?"

Tori blinked because she wasn't sure she'd heard what she thought she had, but before she could speak Jeremiah squeezed her knee to get her attention.

"I love you, honey. Will you marry me?"

She opened her mouth but closed it again when Bryant palmed her cheek, turning her gently to face him.

"I love you so much, darlin'. Please marry me?"

Tori was so overcome with emotions she couldn't speak and tears burned the back of her eyes and then formed and spilled over onto the cheeks. She was just glad that she didn't need to ask the questions the other women involved in the ménage marriages and relationships had, because the women kindly explained how a marriage to more than one man worked. The woman married the oldest man. All she had to do was answer.

"Yes."

Bryant smiled and kissed her lips. "You've made me very happy, darlin'."

"Thank you, honey." Jeremiah hugged her tight and kissed her belly through her robe.

Luther tugged lightly on her ponytail. "Thank you, baby. I love you so fucking much."

"I love you all, too."

Luther reached behind him and when he brought his hand back around to the front, he was holding a small open jewelry box in his hand. Tori covered her mouth and the tears flowed faster. Inside the box was the most beautiful ring she'd ever seen. There was a large baguette diamond in the center and two smaller baguette diamonds were on either side. The platinum band was also covered in diamonds.

"Oh. My. God," she whispered. "It's beautiful."

"Not as beautiful as you are, gorgeous," Luther said while he removed the ring from the box. All three of her men held a small bit of her hand and then Luther slid the ring onto her finger.

"How's the fit, honey?" Jeremiah asked.

"Perfect. Just like my three men."

"We are far from perfect, darlin'," Bryant said.

"You are to me," Tori replied.

Luther scooped her up into his arms and carried her toward the bedroom, with Jeremiah and Bryant hurrying after them.

She knew her men weren't perfect and neither was she. And she knew they would have their arguments and butt heads every now and then, but to her they were the most perfect men she had ever met. They were handsome and sexy and had bodies to die for. But most importantly they loved her and she loved them, and nothing else really mattered.

If they had their love for each other then they could work through any problem and still stand strong.

She'd never imagined a fresh start in life would have led her to meeting the men of her dreams.

Tori was looking forward to spending many years working, living, and loving with her men by her side.

And hopefully in the not too distant future, there would be babies, too.

THE END

WWW.BECCAVAN-EROTICROMANCE.COM

ABOUT THE AUTHOR

My name is Becca Van. I live in Australia with my wonderful hubby of many years, as well as my two children.

I read my first romance, which I found in the school library, at the age of thirteen and haven't stopped reading them since. It is so wonderful to know that love is still alive and strong when there seems to be so much conflict in the world.

I dreamed of writing my own book one day but, unfortunately, didn't follow my dream for many years. But once I started I knew writing was what I wanted to continue doing.

I love to escape from the world and curl up with a good romance, to see how the characters unfold and conflict is dealt with. I have read many books and love all facets of the romance genre, from historical to erotic romance. I am a sucker for a happy ending.

For all titles by Becca Van, please visit
www.bookstrand.com/becca-van

Siren Publishing, Inc.
www.SirenPublishing.com

CPSIA information can be obtained at www.ICGtesting.com
Printed in the USA
BVOW08s0041120315

391285BV00020B/236/P